M000165357

At the Water's Edge

At the Water's Edge

Pradeep Jeganathan

South Focus Press

Published in the United States by
South Focus Press
244 Fifth Avenue, Suite 2802
New York, New York 10001
www.southfocuspress.org

Cover photograph by Pradeep Jeganathan.
Author photograph by Malathi de Alwis.

ISBN 0-9748839-0-5

Contents

The Front Row

The seats in the front were better than those in the back. First, because you could see and hear the teacher better, and also, because the benches weren't wobbly like those at the back of the classroom. But mostly, the tops of the long desks at the back weren't smooth; they had little trenches in them where children had cut their names and shallower but broader cuts made as they etched away at their frustration. This unevenness made your letters go wiggly if you wrote in a thin exercise book.

"If you want to get a good seat in front for the rest of the year, go early to school tomorrow," Krishna's mother had said the night before, and he'd known she was right. He got to school at 6:45 in the morning, 45 minutes before school began. Krishna could walk to King's College in five minutes from Mountbatten Crescent where he lived; lots of the boys lived far away, and spent a lot of time commuting on buses and trains that were crowded and unreliable. Still, by the time class began all the seats were full.

Krishna was in the front row, trying to get used to the new room that was the seventh grade classroom. The walls were coated with *hunu*, which gave them a rough texture and a bright white color. Pasted all over the walls, all around, were brightly colored posters and maps from last year's class. There were several of the human body — cross sections of hearts and lungs, livers and intestines; and various maps of Sri Lanka, in blue, green and yellow. Between the windows of the right hand wall was a large calendar, the days crossed off until the 17th of December, the last school day of the previous year: 1974.

On the wall above the blackboard was the national flag: a fierce gold lion glowing on a blood red cloth. In the lion's paw was a naked sword. On the back wall was a mural of the medieval battle between the two kings Duttu-Gamunu and Elara. Duttu-Gamunu's army was lighter skinned than Elara's. The two kings were atop elephants, and the darker-skinned warrior, Elara, was bleeding badly. On his shield was a tiger. At the side of the victor was a Buddhist monk, holding aloft another gold and crimson lion flag.

Krishna breathed deeply, trying to calm himself, looking away from the mural. Recently, he had been getting attacks of asthma more and more frequently and his father had delved deep into one of his medical textbooks and given him breathing exercises to strengthen his lungs. Krishna exhaled, thinking of the *ana-pana-sati* breathing meditation he had learnt last year in school. It wasn't that different, he thought. Anyway, breathing deeply calmed him when he did it each morning on his bed at home, watching the soft colors of the refracted sun that shone through the windows of his bedroom.

The teacher came in. Dressed in a white cloth and a long white shirt — what they called 'national'— he stood out brightly in front of the freshly cleaned blackboard. His thin black mustache almost blended with his dark upper lip. He kept his bag on the large, solid wooden table in front of the class.

The class greeted him in unison, "*Ayubowan*, sir."

"*Ayubowan*," he said, in Sinhala, holding his hands together.

"Now we will recall our religions for a moment," he continued, and led them in the chant most knew so well: "May all beings be free of sorrow, free of illness, may they be healed... " The Christian boys were quiet, hands crossed behind their backs, eyes lowered, but Krishna joined in the chanting, feeling calm and collected. He liked being

11

a Buddhist. His Hindu parents hadn't been upset when he had said he wanted to change his religion, even though his relatives had been outraged when they heard of it.

Next to Krishna in the front row was Lal. Lal lived a few miles away, but Krishna knew Lal's father had driven him to school; it had been easy for him to come in early. His clothes looked freshly washed and ironed, unlike the shirts and trousers of the other boys that were already sweaty and grimy from long bus rides. He was chanting the stanzas too; his parents were active Buddhists, who always financed the annual *pirith* festival at school, the grandness of which was noticed and appreciated by lots of the teachers.

The religious observations over, the teacher, Mr. Dharmadasa, sat behind his table on his high-backed chair, his left hand circling the spiral at the end of the arm rest. He began reading out the names in the register. Each boy stood up when his name was called so that he could be marked present and the teacher could learn his name. He droned on, going down the list, lifting his eyes as each boy rose and sat again. "Nikamal Balasuriya, Lal Edirishinha, Anura Gajanayake,... H.D. Rohana."

Rohana got up from his seat at the back of the class. Lal giggled from his seat in the front row, loud and confident. He turned and whispered to Krishna in English, "He has a servant's name."

Krishna heard him, but didn't reply, thinking that wasn't right to say. The other boys turned back, almost in unison, to look at Rohana.

Rohana was looking down. Lal had laughed because Rohana didn't have a first and last name like most other boys. The way his name was put together was different; it was fashioned in a sort of rural way with the name of his village preceding his own given name.

Rohana's face, burned dark brown by the sun, grew darker. He had a forced smile on his face, but Krishna could see that his fingers were pressed onto the table and his nails were moving on the surface. He was short; face oily and pock-marked with patches of lighter colored skin on his neck and chin, sweat showing on the sleeves of his shirt where it met his body. His shirt was creased and stretched, and one button was a safety pin.

"Ah! Rohana," the teacher said, ignoring Lal. He continued down the list. "Yugg Yoganadham," He called. There were giggles at the strange name. Krishna stood up. "Say your name," the teacher said, in Sinhala.

"Yoganathan, sir," Krishna said.

"Ah!" The teacher opened his mouth to speak and then stopped himself. He put on his glasses and looked at the register again.

Then very quietly and gently he asked, "*Oya* 'Tamil' *da*?" Self-consciously he replaced the

13

usual Sinhala word *Demala* with the English word Tamil.

"Yes sir," Krishna replied in Sinhala.

"Did you study in Sinhala right from the beginning?" the teacher asked.

"Yes sir."

"Is that allowed?" the teacher wondered softly.

"It was my parents' choice."

"Are both your parents Tamil?"

"Yes sir."

"You didn't have any problems with the language?"

"No sir."

"You have siblings?"

"Yes sir."

"And they are in the Sinhala class also?"

"Yes sir."

"Good, very good." Mr. Dharmadasa nodded, and closed the register, for Krishna's had been the last name. *Demala* was the usual word in Sinhala for a Tamil but Krishna's Sinhala speaking teachers would rarely use it when they talked to him. Krishna liked it when they used the English word. It made him feel accepted, a friend not an enemy.

After finishing with the register Mr. Dharmadasa said, "We must now appoint a monitor. Who was the monitor last year?" he asked.

"We weren't together in the same class," said Lal, "but in my class I was the monitor." They had mixed-up the parallel classes at the end of the sixth grade, as they did every so often.

"I see," the teacher said. "Anyone else?" He looked around thoughtfully, his eyes resting on the boys who were well dressed. "I, sir," came the cry, from several places in the room.

Lal's friend Anura was louder than the others.

"We were monitors together, sir," Lal said, pointing at Anura. Anura was sitting in the fourth row of the class. He was dressed as well as Lal. But his father's car had broken down on the way to school, so he had only come in at 7:25.

Lal and Anura were appointed head and assistant head monitor, respectively. Four others were appointed house monitors. Most of them had been monitors before.

Before starting the day's lessons there was something else to be taken care of. "The class needs a cane," The teacher said, smiling thinly. "Who will buy a cane?"

"I will bring a cane, sir," answered Lal.

The next day, along with the cane, Lal brought a little mechanical game to school. It was a tiny white plastic maze, covered with a transparent plastic top. You had to maneuver the three, dainty shining silver balls, through the maze into the space

15

at the center, by tilting it gently, to and fro. His father had got it for him in Singapore. No one in class had seen anything like it before. Everyone wanted to play with it.

Since the Social Studies teacher was absent that day, the class had a free period. Soon Anura was sharing Lal's seat in the front of the class so they could play with the toy together. This cramped Krishna who was sitting next to Lal on the bench. Krishna was angry with Lal because he hadn't let him play the game. He took his bag, which he usually kept at his feet, and placed it as a barrier between Anura and himself. This further reduced the space on the bench as the bag was full and thick.

"Don't come any closer than this," Krishna said to Anura, his hands on his bag.

"Take that ugly bag away," Anura replied. "There isn't room for it."

"No, there is room for my bag, but there isn't any room for you," said Krishna.

Anura stopped playing the game, turned towards Krishna, put his hands on the bag and started pushing. Krishna pushed back. Just then the teacher from the next class walked in.

"You boys are making far to much noise," he said.

Seeing Anura and Krishna he said, "What are you two trying to do?"

Anura stood up.

"Is this your seat?" he asked Anura. Anura was silent.

"Get back to your seat, right now," the teacher said angrily and walked out of the class. Krishna could see a long cane in the teacher's hands, which were clasped behind his back. He ran up to him, his shoes skidding in the fine sand scattered on the cement floor.

"May I go to the bathroom, sir?" he asked the teacher.

"Yes, you may."

He sped off, pleased that he had avoided asking Lal, the monitor, for permission.

Anura went back to his seat, after borrowing the toy from Lal. Rohana, who was sitting behind him, peered over his shoulder. "Will you give it to me when you are done?" he asked.

"We'll see," said Anura. "Lal may want it back soon. That *Demalaya* is nothing but a pain," he went on, still smarting from the teacher's reprimand.

"What a dog," agreed Rohana.

"Yes," said Anura, "why should he catch a good seat in front?"

"If you give them a little bit they will ask for everything, that's what my father always says," said Rohana.

"They are always grabbing too much, that's the problem," Anura added, "we should teach him a lesson during the interval."

"We want to sit in front too," Rohana told Krishna during the interval.

"You should have come early yesterday, then," replied Krishna.

Rohana's jaw tightened.

"It's the same thing every year," he said. "'Come early', the rich boys say. It's easy for you rich people with your cars. Do you know how long it takes me to get to school? Two hours, and sometimes the bus doesn't even come."

"But I didn't come by car," protested Krishna.

"What lies" Rohana retorted, "all you *Demallu* have plenty of money."

In the back of his mind Krishna had known it was coming, the dreaded word. If he hadn't known the Sinhala people so well it wouldn't have hurt as much. But he knew what the word meant to them. He turned and faced Rohana, wishing the mural wasn't on the wall.

"Shut up," he told Rohana.

"You can't tell me to shut up, you black-lowlife-alien *Demalaya*."

"My family's lived here for thousands of years, as long as the Sinhala have, and what's more

18

you are blacker then a crow," replied Krishna who was light complexioned.

"No!" shouted Rohana, "This is our land, the Sinhala Land, and we have to clean out scum like you. Prince Duttu-Gamunu did it before," he pointed at the wall, "He beat up your *jathiya*, and threw them out and cleaned-up the country. But that was a long time ago, and we will lose the little we have now if we don't do it again."

Krishna stared at the mural speechless, the sweat dripping from his neck, down his back.

They said the *Demala* invaders had destroyed the Buddhist temples, burnt holy books and killed monks. But that was long ago, Krishna thought, and anyhow he was a Buddhist, wasn't he?

"Don't come too much with us," Rohana went on, his voice trembling. "We are Lion-cubs."

Krishna clenched his fist and hit Rohana on the jaw.

And then they were fighting, the class cheering Rohana on, calling him Duttu-Gamunu, and Krishna, Elara.

They were so engrossed in the fight that they didn't hear the bell ring at the end of the interval. Mr. Dharmadasa looked very stern when he walked in.

"Why are you two behaving like animals?" he snapped.

"It's a Sinhala-*Demala* riot," Lal said smiling. "Krishna hit Rohana."

Mr. Dharmadasa turned towards Krishna.

"But... but he called me Elara," said Krishna, softly, as if this were something private. He was too ashamed to say that Rohana had called him *Demalaya*. And he knew he couldn't explain why it was such an insult.

"Sit down everybody. There is no need to be uncivilized and hit each other," said Mr. Dharmadasa. "We should not lose our tempers like this. I will cane you both if I catch you fighting again, we can't have little Duttu-Gamunu Elara fights like this."

He paused to take a breath. "We must all live in peace and harmony in this country, like brothers. It is our tradition. We the Sinhala have always been hospitable to the foreign races. Why, some of my best friends are Tamil." He stopped, looked around, and shook his head.

"The trouble with this class is that it is too undisciplined and noisy. The teacher next-door Mr. Ratnayake, was just complaining to me. I felt ashamed of you boys. The monitors should keep the class quiet when a teacher is absent. Where are those people I appointed as monitors? Why can't you maintain discipline in the class?" Lal and Anura lowered their eyes.

"All these quarrels about sitting in front. I will assign seats to everyone, and that will be final." he said. "The monitors will sit in the front row, so that they can keep the class quiet."

The Watch

The day after the White *dorai* left, Nadesan *dorai* moved in.

The White *dorai* had given Valli's father a watch. It was a real watch with a band of silver links, a gold face, silver hands that moved slowly, and a darker, faster hand Valli could hear ticking at night as she tossed and turned on her straw mat.

Briggs *dorai* had given her father— who was his gardener— the watch the day he left for England. They were in the garden, on the lawn framed by rose bushes. Her father, whose head barely reached the *dorai's* shoulder, stood twisting his body towel in his hands. The black centers of his eyes had gone gray with time, while the whites had turned ocher and red. The *dorai's* white canvas shoes sank into the mud that was oozing up between her father's toes.

"Hope we meet again some time, Mu`taya" he had said, in accented Tamil, to her father who was looking down at the *dorai's* massive thighs. "Take good care of the garden, and be good to your wife and children. I told Nadesan *dorai* that you are a hard worker, and that the lady has trained you personally." Her father looked up at the *dorai*, whose white pith hat was shining in the sun. Then, rubbing the black and gray stubble on his cheek, he said, "I will do my best."

It was then that the *dorai* gave her father the watch, looking a little uncomfortable with the whole thing. As he was walking away he looked back. "Oh! By the way," he said, "Mrs. Nadesan needs a servant girl for her Colombo bungalow. So look around for a good girl, will you?"

*   *

Valli stood in the door of the line room holding the bundle of firewood she had gathered, breathing the smell from the latrines across the narrow path that wafted through the door. Her father was squatting in the far corner of their one-roomed shack. He was balancing his tin plate in one hand, eating the rice and dhal with the other. Her mother was bending over his plate, serving him coconut sambol.

He was yelling at her, as he ate. "In God's name, woman, she's fourteen— old enough to be married in the old days."

"But I need her to help me with the two boys and the kitchen work."

"Nonsense! You don't need help with those things. That is your work, a woman's work. You managed fine when she was little. And don't tell me that you get tired out from plucking tea; I work hard too."

"But to go to Colombo, all alone— what will happen if she fell ill again?"

"She's not going to be all alone, you fool. The *dorai's* wife will be there. I have to do this; the Briggs *dorai* asked me himself when he gave me the watch. Also, it will be an insult to the new *dorai* if I say no. We must make a good impression on him; he mustn't think we are getting uppity ideas from the trade union people."

*   *

Nadesan, the new manager of the West-green tea estate, had just been had transferred to Nuwara-Elliya, from Hatton, where he had been stationed before. It was a move up, to a bigger estate — Eastcliffe was replacing all its British managers with locals. Not a moment too soon, thought Nadesan, it was more than twenty fives years since independence, even though the talk of a government take over of the sterling companies worried him. Won't happen, he thought; glad more than ever to have the estate bungalow near Nuwara-Elliya, especially in the season, when everyone from Colombo would come up for the races. His family came up during the children's school holidays this year, and his nephews Krishna and Suresh who'd come up also, had had a nice time. Tomorrow he'd drive all of them back to Colombo. His wife Kamala and the children would remain in their house on Mountbatten Crescent that she ran, so that Sonali and Ramesh could go to schools there: Queen's and King's.

*   *

Valli sat at the edge of the back seat of the car, squeezing herself against the door. She kept her knees close together so that the children would have more room. Her left palm was plastered against the door. It was a small car, making it a tight fit for the five at the back. But Ramesh, who wasn't very heavy, was asleep on Krishna's lap, while Suresh sat forward, making room for Sonali.

Valli's plait of hair was blowing in the wind, the red ribbon at the end flapping along. She kept her eyes lowered to shield them from the fine dust that sprayed in through the window as they

26

drove along the winding mountain road from Nu-wara-Elliya to Colombo. On her forehead was a black *pottu* mark; Mrs. Nadesan wore a red one since she was married. The sunlight fell on Valli's calves; she pulled down her thin skirt again and glanced at the children. Their legs were smooth, the brown skin shining with a healthy sheen.

Suresh whispered something to Krishna, who shrugged. Undeterred, he whispered to Sonali. She tilted her head, and looked down.

"*Amma*, why are her legs full of spots?" Sonali sang out in English to her mother, who was sitting in front.

"Who, darling? Oh the girl? She must have had sores. That's what will happen to you if you don't wash yourself properly," Mrs. Nadesan said ominously. Mr. Nadesan chuckled as he slowed down to take another bend in the road.

Valli sensed what they were talking about, even though she hardly knew English. She remembered the fever that had given her the marks. She had been lying on her mat for many days, her eyes following the bumps on the sheet metal roof. It had taken a long time to get a van to take her to the hospital, and then her mother had pawned her gold *thaali* to buy the medicine.

*　　　　　　　　　　　　　　　　*

27

She rubbed the carbolic soap the lady had given her on her legs, starting from her thighs. Then she took a piece of coconut husk from the shelf, wet it and for the second time that day scrubbed down her calves. Next, she took the smooth round stone she had found in the garden and weighed it in her palm. Her mother used a similar stone for the more stubborn stains on their clothes. She rubbed her legs with it, slowly at first, using circular strokes at the scars, harder and faster with every stroke until the skin broke and the stone was bloody.

*   *

Three thirty was tea time at the Nadesans — and often Mrs. Yoganathan from next door, and some times Mrs. Wickramasinghe from down the road, would join the lady and the children for cake and tea. Valli served the yellow cake, after cutting thin slices in the kitchen, on a small white plate — the tea on a silver tray, in a light blue pot, with a jug of warm milk, a bowl of sugar, and matching cups with tiny silver spoons.

The French windows of the living room, opened out onto a smooth green lawn — but Valli's eyes always moved from the sloping vista to linger on the beautiful framed picture on the far wall of the room where a lady dressed like her mother was plucking tea. She looked happy, smiling, lips painted bright red, her eyes lined, and lashes thickened. And she wasn't sweating. Mrs. Nadesan had told Valli that the English letters at the bottom of the poster, was the name of Briggs *dorai's* company.

When Valli's mother would come home from work on the estate, dizzy from the sun, her gums dark with betel, the corn on her right forefinger inflamed from plucking and plucking, her neck swollen and stiff — she would always call Valli to rub her back, while the pot boiled for tea. Suddenly the l—ady called out, "don't day dream girl," and Valli turned and hurried forward with the tea tray, eyes lowered.

"So you've got a nice new girl, Kamala?" said Mrs. Wickramasinghe.

Mrs. Nadesan nodded. "Yes, we got her from the estate," she said, glancing at Valli.

"Kamalakka, you are so lucky — it is so hard to get servants these days," Mrs. Yoganathan smiled at her elder sister.

"Ahh! But I've had to train her from scratch, don't forget — she didn't know any thing, never worked in a bungalow before."

"Such a lot of work, no?" Mrs. Wickramasinghe clucked sympathetically, "Still she is young, that is good, easier to train."

"I think she will work out; she is picking up the work fast."

29

Mrs. Nadesan nodded, as the three ladies turned to Valli, who had laid the tea things down, and was pouring, her dark hair braided and coiled on the nape of her neck.

"She has put on since you got her, no, Kamalakka?" asked Mrs. Yoganathan.

Her sister chuckled, "Yes, I also noticed. Getting three meals a day, for a change."

Valli finished, and stood by the lower table, eyes lowered, not moving, sensing they were speaking about her, her face flushing slowly.

"She is developing, I can see," Mrs. Wickramasinghe nodded, considering, eyes on the girl's chest, which was rising and falling with each breath.

Mrs. Nadesan nodded, again, and smiled. "Will have to be careful, soon. Or she will be running after all the servant boys and drivers down the road, trying to get pregnant and what not."

They all laughed delicately and nodded, while Mrs. Nadesan turned to Valli, and asked, "Valli, have you finished sewing the hems on the curtains?"

"Yes lady."

Mrs. Nadesan smiled kindly. "Ah! You have finished so fast, very good. You can have piece of cake with your tea today."

Valli felt the fan whirling overhead, churning the air, cooling her, as she turned to go back to the kitchen, her steps slowing as her toes sank into the soft carpet on the floor. She longed for the cool mountain air of Nuwara-Elliya — and she liked the breeze from the living room fan. There wasn't one in the kitchen. At night, after all the dinner dishes were washed, and she had eaten what she was given in the kitchen, she rolled aside the carpet in the living room, and lay her mat to sleep, since the cook slept in the small servant's room off the kitchen. The first day, she had turned the fan right up to 5 before she slept, but the lady had said electricity was too expensive for a fan all night.

*   *

"Do you know where my facecream is?" asked Mrs. Nadesan.

"I didn't take it," answered Valli quickly.

"I didn't say you took it — and come away from that wall, don't clutch it. How many times do I have to tell you this, you don't have to hold it, it won't fall down you know. And now there are dirty patches on every wall because of this — Ah! Here it is," she said picking up the glass jar from the edge of the dressing table. "It is nearly empty," she exclaimed. "Do you know any thing about this?"

"No, I don't even know what it is."

"Look child, you have seen me use this cream on my face, haven't you?"

Valli looked down guiltily. She had seen the lady use it at night, masking her face with it, looking like a ghost. But in the morning her skin would look so clear and smooth highlighting her white teeth and her heavy gold *thaali* she wore around her neck. Valli had thought the cream would work for her too.

"It is a very expensive cream which I get specially made for my type of skin," Mrs. Nadesan paused waiting for a confession. "You stole it, didn't you?" she said angrily.

"No, I didn't — I don't need your cream."

'Don't be cheeky you *thotta kadu* girl," She spat out the words and slapped Valli on the face. "You will have to pay for the cream from your salary. I will deduct ten rupees every month."

*   *

"Now that you've worked a month, you can buy some cloth to make a new skirt and blouse," Mrs. Nadesan told Valli. Valli took the money the lady gave her, folded it into a small wad, tied her handkerchief tightly around it, and thrust it deep into her blouse.

The store looked crowded and noisy from outside. Valli's pulse quickened as they walked in; she knew what she wanted to buy. Inside, the fat man in the crisp, nylon shirt twitched his shoulders and settled into his high stool by the counter.

"It is a very good material," he said, looking at the dark green bolt of cloth Valli was pointing to. "Imported." He reached out his wooden yardstick, then with a little toss and a twist picked out the roll from the multicoloured stack on the shelf. "But a little expensive," he added scowling gently at her.

"You really want that one?" asked Mrs. Nadesan. "It is too thick for a skirt, what will you make from it?" Valli was silent, looking down. "Well, buy it if you want to, it's your money," Mrs. Nadesan said grudgingly.

The next week Mrs. Nadesan said, "I'm going to the tailor's tomorrow. You can come along if you want your new out fit made."

Valli smiled and nodded.

"You can draw a sketch of what you want, so that it is easy to explain. Do you want a blouse as well?"

"Yes, lady."

"Well show me a sketch when you have done it, so that I can see if you have enough cloth for it."

*   *

33

"A what?!" the Lady exclaimed. "A 'Trouser suit'" Valli repeated, saying the words diffidently in English. "Like the young lady has." She wanted a pair of tailored slacks, and tunic top, just like Sonali had. Then her legs and arms wouldn't show, and the scars would be hidden.

"You want to wear a trouser suit and prance about, one would think you are the lady of the house. You must be mad, totally mad!"

And later on the phone to Nuwara-Elliya, she spoke with her husband, " ...and she was coming along so nicely, learning the work so quickly, and then this... I was going give her a new skirt and blouse for *Dheepavali*..."

*   *

Valli lay with her stomach on the mat, the cross-woven straw making patterns on her knees. Her father, she knew, kept the watch on the table near where he slept. She could feel the watch in her hand now as she took it out of the blue velvet case. Down by the stream, where no one would hear her, she would open the strap out, lay it out on the flat stone they washed clothes on, and pound it with a hard rock, until the links broke, the glass face shattered and the smithereens vanished into the sand.

The Street

The men ran towards the cars as they slowed down at the traffic light. The *mahatturu* in the cars lowered their windows to look at the bunches of *rambuttans* the men held up. If they liked the look of them they would taste one, breaking the furry red outer cover with a quick bite, spitting it out quickly and then sucking, nipping and licking on the white meat on the nut, lips wet with the clear sour-sweet juice.

Then came the bargaining. You had to be quick, the traffic lights changed fast. The cars moved on and you readied yourself for the next red light. It wasn't always *rambuttans*— other kinds of fruit if they were cheap or in season— grapes, some times. Or packets of cashew nuts. Once they had tried large prawns, holding them high in bunches. Karuna remembered the rhythm, and the cracks and edges of the pavement on her feet, as she had run up and down, helping Piyasena when business was good. But he had stopped selling things after the car had hit him five years ago. He had only been in hospital for a few days, it hadn't been such a big thing, but he had stopped.

Today Karuna stood alone at the junction trying to hear the woman over the noise of the traffic. "So put the children in a *madama*," the woman selling earrings had said, the loose flesh on her arms moving with a life of its own, "I'll find a place for them like this." She snapped her fingers to show how easy it was going to be. "I know a *mahattaya* who knows about things like this." She pursed her lips and nodded wisely.

Karuna who had told her story in little spurts between deep breaths looked skeptical. "Then I won't see them again," she said.

"No, no." Kaluamma pacified her, "in this *madama* they will be looked after very well, and you can see them any time. Just what you need. Leave your man," she went on, "the beater of women, I bet he can't even stand up to a Tamil. With weaklings like him around, it's no wonder the Tamils are beating the Sinhala up."

She eyed Karuna speculatively. "He can't do it any more, can he? Karuna nodded, biting her lip shyly.

"Don't worry about the children." Kaluamma said. "I got my cousin's friend's children into the Thavutissa *madama* last week. That one is a very good *madama*, run by the famous Balasuriya *mahattaya*. He is so noble and generous — a perfect *mahattaya*. My *mahattaya* knows him well; your children will come out really posh; like proper *mahatturu* and *nonala* from that one. Just a little money and I will arrange the rest," she said fingering the small wad of notes tucked into the waistline of her cloth. "But come-on, why should you be drying yourself out in the sun," She patted the worn yellow mat beside her — "Come sit in the shade with me. Now what about a pair of earrings for you?"

"No, no, I don't have any money for things like that."

"Tell me which one you want— I don't want any money," said Kaluamma, expanding her chest generously.

Karuna looked at the little cart that housed Kaluamma's collection. In it were hundreds of earrings, small gold studs, big red rings, earrings set with blue and green stones — they were as good as anything she had seen in Dubai. Karuna hadn't bought a pair when she was working there because she wanted to save all the money she could. But now she could have a pair for free. Slowly, her eyes went from earring to earring, savoring the pleasure of choice. Now and then she bent to caress an especially lovely pair. "These are nice," she said finally,

37

cradling a pair in her hot palm. "Are they too expensive?" she asked diffidently.

"Oh, these are very fine. I can see you have a good eye. It is almost real gold — did you know that? And see how delicate these hanging gold chains are."

Kaluamma held the earrings to Karuna's ears. Her hands felt rough against Karuna's soft lobes. She could feel the little chains brush the side of her neck.

"Delicate but strong," Kaluamma went on, "you couldn't break them if you wanted to; you will have them for a long time." She released Karuna from her grasp then, weighing the earrings in her hands, added, "But you can have them free." And she snapped her knuckles as she did when she made a good sale. "You are going to look very nice in them," she went on smiling, "a little lipstick and you will be perfect. My *mahattaya* might even have a job for you."

*   *

Karuna was combing Sudu's hair as she hissed urgently to wake her other daughter. She wanted them up and off to school before Piyasena woke up and rose from the cardboard bed. Her back blocked the faint morning light from touching his face. There were no other openings in the cardboard walls of the shack; but even so the water found its way in when it rained hard. Piyasena was sleeping on his back, his chest exposed. She could see the old tattoo on his chest that she had liked so much when she had first known him. 'My only treasure is my mother' it said, the black letters now blending into his brown skin.

His arms had felt like iron rods as they smashed into her flesh the day before. She screamed she didn't have the money he wanted. But he didn't believe her. He said he wanted to sell *rambuttans* at the junction again. But she knew he would spend it on drink as he had all the other money she had saved. "I don't have any money," she wailed over and over again, keeping her eyes averted from Kota's big school textbook, where she had hidden the last of the Dubai money.

Then he picked up the *manna*. And he raised it to bring it crashing down on her. She ran straight into him — clutching the big knife — pushing down. The knife cut him. Blood spurted from his chest. She had never done that before. Afraid he might kill her for it, she ran out onto the road and all the way to the traffic lights. Out of breath, looking back over her shoulder every few minutes, she had stopped near the earring-woman.

This was the first time he had done something like this after she had come back from Dubai. In the first few months after her return he had been so gentle, just like he had been when they had first been together, that she really thought he had changed back to his old self.

Before she went away he had broken her nose. He would be waiting for her, seething, when she came back from working at the Wickramasinghe bungalow, the slightest little thing setting him off. She didn't know what he knew or didn't, but she could sense he had heard some thing on the street. It was then that she had decided to stop working there and try the Dubai job. But he had disliked that idea even more.

Too ashamed to tell the doctor who stitched her up what had really happened she made up a story about falling into the canal. But this time she had blurted out her story to Kaluamma.

        *   *

"So you are back, huh?" Wickramasinghe *nona* examined her like a picture. "Looking quite different too. Not like when you used to work in my kitchen." She laughed, as if remembering. "You might almost be a *nona* yourself now."

Karuna smiled submissively, and stared at her feet hoping she looked contrite enough. It had been a long walk to Mountbatten Crescent, from the *watte*. She didn't want the *nona* irritated with her today.

"So when did you come back?"

"It is a few months, *nona*."

"And you didn't come to see us?"

"I have been looking to come, *nona*."

"And how long were you there?"

"About a year, *nona*," Karuna counted the months on her fingers, saying each out aloud, softly. "I went in January '85."

"So you must know foreign cooking now, aah? When are you going back to work for Dubai *nonala*?"

"Anay, I don't know *nona*— I can't do anything because of the children. Their father didn't send them to school when I was away: he put them to work at the Goonesekere house down the road. There is no one to look after them in the *watte*." She paused, shifting her weight from one foot to the other. "I came to ask you if you could get the girls into a *madama* for me."

The *mahattaya* walked slowly onto the verandah. He walked with his heavy upper body bent slightly forward, taking steps that seemed full and lumbering, but still kept him from moving forward. His body swayed very slightly, as he stood and his upper arms flexed, as if they were happy to do nothing. He looked at her lazily with the familiar glance she remembered so well and Karuna felt her earlobes burn, the heat running down into the gold chains fixed on her ears. She lowered her eyes, and

41

tried to turn her head in a futile attempt to hide the earrings; she wished she had worn the old, plain studs instead.

"She wants to put her children in a *madama*," the *nona* told Mr. Wickramasinghe.

He looked her up and down again. "A woman should look after her children. What is the world coming to? She has got all these ideas from her foreign jaunts, no?"

"It is a magic word for these people — *madama*. You get rid of the children and live happily ever after," Mrs. Wickramasinghe went on.

"Why do you want to do this?" the *mahattaya* barked at Karuna.

"If the children are safe, I can leave the *watte*. I can work in a house and live there. I can't live with my man any more; I have taken enough." She paused. Her right arm pressed across her body, clutching her left arm at the elbow. She spoke in a rush stumbling over the words. "He beats me, and when he is angry I'm afraid he will kill me."

She looked up at them for a moment, but their eyes were cold. "And he hit and cut me with the *manna* yesterday."

"Really?" said the *nona*. "Where?"

"Here." She said vaguely, her hand going to her chest. She could see that the *nona* didn't believe her.

42

"Well the wound won't heal if you wear such a tight dress, will it?" The *nona* said.

It was the *mahattaya's* turn. "You must try to live in peace and harmony with your man; without making him angry. Remember, the family is one of the building blocks of our society; if you break up your family it will be bad for our society. And what is more, no good will come to you." He inhaled as if he had been emptied of everything he knew and needed replenishing. "So give up this idea of a *madama*. Anyway they are overflowing with orphans; there is no room for children who have parents." He looked her up and down again. "You can come and work here," he added.

"No, no I'll send for you if I need you," said the *nona*, looking at him sharply.

They turned to leave. "I will go then." Karuna bowed her head, and got a nod in return. She could hear them talk as they were walking indoors. "Did you see how she was all tarted up, with her finger nails painted and all that. She probably has another man she wants to shack up with— that is why she wants to give the children away."

"And another thing," said the *mahattaya*. "She must be acting big with her Dubai stories and irritating her man."

*   *

43

"And this was my room in the house where I worked." Karuna was showing her daughters Sudu and Kota the photographs from Dubai. Their eyes moved slowly across the picture, from the long mirror on the wall to the white sheets on the bed. "You had this room all to yourself?" asked Kota with disbelief. This was not the first time they had looked at the photographs. Every so often the girls would want to see them again, and after they had asked many times Karuna would give in. She would take out her suitcase, which served as a prop for the cardboard bed, and find the album among her other mementos. "Did they let you sleep on that bed every..." Sudu stopped and looked up, frightened.

Piyasena was standing at the door. Karuna knew he was drunk. "Put that good for nothing book away, you whore," he screamed. Karuna dropped the album, and slowly backed into a corner.

That's right *putha* you tell her." It was Piyasena's mother who lived in the adjoining shanty. Rosalin had raised five children and never tired of telling the world about it. "She has been bad luck ever since you brought her. I told you at the very beginning but you wouldn't listen." Rosalin was shouting again. "That she-devil must have cast a vicious charm on all of us. That is why you had that accident. And now you can't even work as a laborer. And look at me — struck down in the prime of life."

She had a stroke and was crippled, but could shout as loud as ever.

"Don't worry about anything," he slurred, "I can handle my woman." He lurched towards her but fell on his face as he lunged. Karuna hurried out with Sudu and Kota, a stream of abuse from Rosalin hitting them as they left.

*   *

Karuna stood very straight on the narrow walk between the hut and the canal. She had just finished washing the clothes and they were in a basket balanced on her head. Piyasena sat on his haunches out in front of the shack. The cut on his chest where the *manna* had hit him was red and raw. "You should get the wound dressed, or it will become poisonous," Karuna said softly.

"Don't tell me what to do, you bitch," he snapped. "Save it for that motherfucker *mahattaya* you give your arse to." He chewed slowly on his wad of *bulath* pushing it from one jaw to the other with his tongue. "Remember that suitcase of yours?" he said, his nostrils flaring.

"Yes?" Karuna was startled.

He spat-out a long stream of *bulath* juice on to her feet. She could feel his hot, thick saliva dripping down between her toes and into the earth below.

"I sold it."

※   ※

Karuna stood at the traffic light junction, looking carefully at every car that passed her. Kaluamma had told her to stand there. "The car will come from the *madama*," she had said. But it was late at night and Karuna didn't feel safe. She stood carefully on the pavement, feeling the breaks and spaces on the surfaces her feet knew well. It was harder today, because she was wearing the very tall shoes with the thin straps that Kaluamma had given her — and she could feel her calves pinching and twitching, as Kota and Sudu tugged at her hands from either side. They each had brown paper bags, with all their belongings.

The traffic lights kept changing, cars pulling up, and then purring off.

A car drove up quietly. "Get in." said the driver. He drove fast and soon she didn't know what road they were on. "Will you come and visit us at the *madama*, *Ammi*?" asked Kota. Karuna put her hand on the girl's head. "Now don't you keep whining for me all the time, *duva*," she said. "Be obedient and do as you are told." The car skidded to a halt. "I'll come whenever I can." She held Sudu's hand.

"Get out," said the driver. "No, just you, not the brats."

The car had stopped at another traffic light junction Karuna didn't know. There was a street-light flickering above, and two pretty girls were standing in the half dark, white light it gave off. "No, no, Kaluamma promised me I would be able to see the *madama*."

"What are you jabbering about? Do you want to work or not?"

"But Kaluamma said…"

"Look, I don't know this Kaluamma, and I don't care what she said. The *mahattaya* said I was to pick you up for work."

"But the *madama* for the children?"

"Ah! the *madama*… ! That will be all taken care of —don't worry about anything— the children will be well looked after. But if you don't work —no *madama*— that is what the *mahattaya* said. If you don't work how will you be able to pay for the *madama*? Don't worry about anything." Karuna was silent, trying not to move. Her earrings felt heavy and the chains scraped her neck.

"Don't try to show me how modest you are— show that to the *mahatturu*, some of them like that." said the driver. "Looks like you'er ready for work, huh?" He turned around and looked at her. His lips curled back, exposing his black teeth. "This is the right job for you," he said.

Sri Lanka

When he turned to the quiet sound of her voice, he knew he'd heard her before, that she had already called out several times, and that she'd reached him somewhere in a recess of his unquiet mind. She was smiling now as he turned, repeating with a tiny hesitant upward inflection — a half question: "Krishna?"

He had just walked into the student center library, the bad cafeteria dinner still sitting heavy in him, looking for the *Island-International*, the newspaper from home that you could check out at the library desk. It wasn't a library newspaper; they didn't get newspapers from home at the library. Someone else, Ravi, a senior he didn't quite know, got it and was kind enough to leave it at the desk for every one else. Today it hadn't been there; it had been checked out. Upset, he hadn't even looked up as he turned to go to the carrels until Ashley's voice had reached him.

"Oh hi!" He said, and then as the realization that she had been saying his name for a while sank in, smiled shyly. "Sorry, I was thinking of something else."

He knew her name; she'd introduced herself the other day after the big panel discussion on Sri Lanka the South-Asia graduate student group had organized. But he stood there, tongue stuck in his mouth, mind emptying out, turning blurred and desolate as the snow covered pavement outside, gazing at Ashley as if she was but a vision from another world. Today she was in a blue sweater, which was thick and soft around her slim form, snuggling her neck in its folds, pressing gently on the lines of her jaw, with sleeves so long that her small hands were almost covered by them, only tiny pink tips peeking out, moving on the edge of the wool.

"Hi," he said again, a familiar feeling of stupidity overcoming him.

She was smiling gently; as if she sensed how he felt. "How are you doing?"

He usually hated that question, it had been his pet peeve all of freshman year —the 'how are you doing?' that didn't mean any thing, that everyone here just threw around. But she asked it differently, making him want to answer.

"I'm... I'm fine, and you?"

"I'm great."

He sat down on the long sofa in the lobby of the library, half turned towards her. The *Island-International* was on her lap, a little crumpled, one corner under her denim encased right thigh.

"I wanted to ask you..." she stopped, and nibbled on her lower lip, wetting it with her tongue, diffident. "I'm trying to write this paper, on Sri Lanka, and I am so confused. I was wondering, could I talk to you about it?"

Krishna glanced up at her face, thinking he shouldn't stare, but not taking his eyes off the smooth, glowing, slightly flushed planes of her cheeks. He met her eyes for an instant, blue gray under darkened lashes.

"Yes, of course. I mean... sure, but I don't think I know enough to help with a paper." He paused and shrugged very slowly.

She laughed softly, almost teasingly. "Aww... I heard you ask that question at the talk; didn't Professor Fulton say it was the best question of the day?"

He flushed dark at that, lowering his eyes. "No, no..." he shook his head. "He was just being encouraging." He remembered the open sea of faces turned back as he had got up to ask the question, expectant, watching, making his heart pound as he spoke. He remembered her face, turned back,

51

framed by her unruly hair, watching him as his words tumbled out, quickly but then smoothly.

Unconsciously, he touched his own lower lip to his teeth.

"Come on, it was a great question. And any way you are from there, right? I mean you know so much more than me."

"Ok." He said, feeling both warm and empty inside himself. "What is your paper about?"

They talked for an hour or so about Ashley's paper. It wasn't all that clear to him, at first, what it was about; but he got the general drift of her interests. The class was on political conflict, and Sri Lanka and Nicaragua were cases they had done. But he was absorbed, and after a few exchanges, he was surprised at how much he did know. He thought all he really knew were differential equations, and Maxwell's laws, so usually he never even dared discuss liberal arts or social science stuff with some one who was actually majoring in it.

"Wow," Ashley said after while. "You've read so much. Are you in Polisci?"

He chuckled at that. "No, I'm 8 & 6-1."

"Six? Oh no... the MIT numbers thing. That is so crazy you know?"

"I know. Sorry, but every thing has a number here. It is crazy. Even more so if it is a double major. 8 is physics. 6-1 is electrical engineering."

"Electrical? Isn't that the hardest one? I mean there is that big class right, in programming? I heard that is a terror?" Ashley went to Wellesley, so MIT for her was a foreign country she was still getting to know.

"Yes, 6001. I'm in that now."

"I bet you are acing it."

He felt his cheeks warm. "I'm... I don't know. I think if you do the problem sets, you are ok." He knew he had to get to work on the next one, which was sitting in his backpack. It had looked long when he had glanced at it before dinner. "Looks like you've got a lot of notes there, Ashley." Her yellow pad was filled with scribblings, points he had made, references he had cited, and then there were special areas on the sheet she'd circled, which contained what she called her "aha points."

"Yep. Lots. Got to get to the computer center. I thought I'd use the one here since the one at Wellesley is so useless."

"Oh here? The student center one? Isn't it rather crowded?"

She sighed, and shrugged, long curls of light hair caressing her right cheek and ear, as she buried herself deeper in the sofa. "Got to wait; it is such a drag."

*   *

It was the next day that he saw her, waiting in the student center computer room, sitting at a table, books spread in front of her, scribbling on her pad. He'd walked into collect a printout he had sent from the cluster where he worked, since the printer there was down.

He stopped by her. "Been waiting long?"

She looked up, almost translucent white teeth showing through her parted lips, as she smiled brightly at him. "Yes, and there is no end in sight. These guys are playing computer games on the terminals." She hissed.

He nodded. "They tend to do that. But, you know what?"

"What?" She grinned, tilting her head up, hands going to her thick, soft hair, pulling it back off her face with a smooth motion.

"You could just use a terminal in the Athena cluster in building 11."

"Eleven?" Ashley went, but she wasn't kidding now. "The one right off the infinity corridor, right?"

"Infinite." He smiled. "Yes, that one."

"Don't you need a key or something to get in?"

"A password. I work there. Come with me, I'll show you."

They stopped at the traffic lights waiting for them to change before they crossed. He glanced up across the road, as he always did, at the cube in the corner that said 77 Massachusetts Avenue, and the huge roman looking columns that dominated the entrance. Krishna had been 14 when he had told himself he would go to MIT, when deep in *Resnick and Halliday*, he had understood Maxwell's laws. They were the most beautiful thing he'd ever known, so wonderful in their elegance that he felt, when he thought of them, he could hold the universe in his hands.

When the light turned amber, he turned to her, seeing the soft flakes of snow, descending, bright in the darkening sky, falling onto her hair, settling in the tendrils and wisps.

"Here." He handed her his scarf.

She looked at it. "What?"

"To cover your hair."

"To cover my hair?" She looked quizzically at him.

"Yes, Oh I mean... from the snow." He looked up, unsure how to be clear. "You need a hat may be?"

"Oh. No, I am always macho about winter." Then she looked at him, head slanted to one side. "That was weird for a moment. I thought you were saying like I need to cover my hair." She laughed knowingly, as she had found him out. "Is that a custom in Sri Lanka?"

"No of course not." He stepped away, sideways, balling the scarf in his hand, walking quickly across the road, as the light changed. He never knew what to say to something like that. You could always say yes or no, but qualifications were needed if you were going to be honest, and qualification were hard. But he knew he'd started reading books on Sri Lanka, because he needed to explain things, to himself and others — because if that world, his world over there had ever made sense, it seemed far more confused when questioned from outside.

He ran up the steps, as he always did, draping the scarf back on his neck, stopping only at the door realizing he'd left Ashley behind. He stopped, and waited for her, stepping aside so that she could walk through the famous old automatic door into the lobby of the Institute. She went through but stopped, not going on. He pointed forward. "This way," he said, thinking she was confused about where they were going.

She didn't move, but looked up at him, hugging her books to her chest, saying again, "Krishna?" so softly, it was a whisper. He saw the look on her face and he stopped short, moving closer.

"Krishna, I'm sorry. I upset you. I didn't mean to."

He felt his back relax and his face smoothen its tightness. "No it is fine. But thank you for saying that. I... some times. I don't know how to explain every thing, ok?"

She leant forward and put her hand on his arm. "I'm just a totally ignorant WASP girl. You've got to remember that." She moved closer, standing inches from him, face lifted, eyes large and open. "You've been so nice to explain things to me. I really appreciate it. Don't be mad okay?" Her fingers moved gently on his arm, and the scent of her hair enveloped him. Suddenly he wanted to kiss her.

"No, no, I'm not mad," he said, shaking his head, and trying to smile. He could feel every male eye that went past flickering on them, on Ashley, she standing so close to him, one glance following the other, drawn it seemed to the glow of her face, and radiance of her hair. He took her hand gently, "come, please."

They stopped at the glass door to the Athena cluster, and he pressed the keys of the electronic combination lock, making it flash, she beside him and quiet.

"It is a bit Sci-Fi like here. But hey... It is MIT, right?"

She laughed softly, eyes meeting his.

He settled her down in front of the large new VX120 workstations; the whole row was vacant, colored patterns spinning idly on the dark curved screens.

"So... But will someone ask me for ID or something?"

The room was empty, except for two guys who were at the far end, hacking away. "Oh no. That is the beauty of this place; no one talks to any one else. No one checks any thing. And especially every one in Athena is 6-3 and way into d&d; you know the kind who wears those light brown glasses indoors?" He grinned. "They are scared of nearly every thing; no way they will even look at you — you'll terrify them."

She laughed at that quietly, but hard. "You are funny." She said. "Thanks so much for this."

He smiled happily, standing up to leave. "Oh it is not a big thing. Now at least you can work in peace."

But it turned out that she didn't know Emacs, the text processor she needed to know to use the Vax, so he had to walk her through the basics, the control xs and control cs.

"Krishna?"

There was a upward slant again, that he was beginning to recognize. He had been checking something out on the system waiting for Ashley to make sure she had mastered the basics of the text processor. He swiveled the dark blue chair to turn to her, loving its contoured comfort, listening.

"You know I understand more of the history of Sri Lanka now, and how the Sinhala Tamil thing developed. But I still don't get the 1983 riots? How come that happened?" She touched her lower lip to her teeth, as if she may have said the wrong thing again, and her face tensed. "I mean I don't know enough, I guess?"

He listened, still, hearing her words. His fingers moved on the cushioned arm rests, nails scraping the cloth. Behind her, the white wall of the room dazzled him, and the row of embedded lights in the ceiling flickered with fierce power.

He forced himself to take his eyes off the wall. "There is this paper I read," He offered, trying to remember and then make sensible what he did. "It had an unusual argument. It isn't the relative deprivation of the lower classes theory that Tambiah offers. I mean I think that is kind of true. But this paper argues that different sections of the capitalist classes benefited differentially from the structural economic reforms the IMF wanted."

Ashley was scribbling in her pad; Krishna didn't really see her fingers move, but he saw the shapes emerge on the yellow sheet.

"Different sections? So how does that become Sinhala vs. Tamil?"

"Some Tamil sections benefited more from the import trade he says. And they then out did their Sinhala competitors. There is more to it, but that is the gist of it. He is a Marxist anthropologist in Sri Lanka, Gunesinghe. You must read his stuff."

"You are such a gold mine. Thanks again." Ashley wrote down the reference that he gave her. "And how on earth do you remember even the publisher? I swear you are a computer!"

He laughed at that, and said nothing for a moment, just basking in the warmth of her praise, "No of course not. I forget loads."

"Lot less than me, I'm sure."

"Well you've got a lots of stuff to remember." He smiled at her teasingly. "Password for the room, for my account, and all the Emacs stuff. You got it all?"

She nodded hand moving on the writing pad.

"Okay, I'll see you around then. Oh and…" He bent and wrote his dorm phone number on the edge of her pad. "You can call from the extension here." He pointed. "Dial 5 and the number. Just in case something goes wrong?" He sensed the unfamiliar upward inflection creep into his voice.

"Thanks so much."

*   *

"Krishna?"

It was a week later that she called; the paper was done and she wanted to thank him. He pressed the phone close to his ear, to make her voice louder, for the line was always bad, but more to feel

60

her closer. His ear traced each little inflection, every tiny pause, and each tinkling laugh almost before he heard them.

He stopped his racing mind, stilling it, speaking in another voice. "Ashley?"

She said "Ye...es?" back as if to tease his serious tone.

"I'd like to ask you to come over for dinner sometime, please?"

He felt calm as he had when he first began to row, when he knew he was one with the oars, and the motion of the boat. He felt his thumb, tight, almost numb on the hand set.

"Sure! Oh I would love that."

"I'll cook?"

"Oh Sri Lankan food? Will you? That would be awesome."

*   *

He started early on Friday, smashing the cloves of garlic with the side of his cleaver, pushing off the thin brittle skin with his thumb, collecting a pile before dicing. It was going to be chicken curry, lentils and rice since Ashley was so excited about Sri Lankan food. He didn't really know how to do it like it was done at home, since he'd never really cooked at home. He'd learnt to cook at MIT, because there were kitchens in the dorm and cafeteria food was so bad; he was working hard on stews since they kept well, and stir fries since they were so quick. But he had kind of got *coq au vin* right a couple times, and some times tried to go a little further. But today he was using his father's recipe, written in neat hand, mailed to him in the kind of notebook you used in school back home; *Appa* had retired, and was now learning how to cook.

He was peeling ginger when Julie walked in, humming, ever present Walkman wrapped around her ears, shrouded in an enormous hooded red sweat shirt that said 'MIT' in big white letters on it.

She stopped by him, and watched.

"Ohh... you are cooking? Looks fancy." She poked at the garlic, taking off her headphone.

He stopped and grinned at Julie. "Nah it is not fancy. Just kind of basic."

Julie was nice, and unfailingly kind; she was a senior, but she had time for every one, always listening and encouraging. She didn't care much for guys as such; she spent a lot of time with all the other female soft ball players. But from time to time she'd check in on Krishna, saying "You thinking of home again?" with unerring accuracy.

She glanced at the place settings on the plain white table in the big common room the kitchen opened into.

"Oh. Company?"

Krishna turned to her, a piece of peeled ginger in the palm of his hand, nude and oblong. "Just a friend." There was something in his voice, and Julie caught it.

"A date? That is way cool." Julie patted his shoulder. "Do I know her?"

"She is at Wellesley. Ashley. She is in Polisci there."

"Not the blonde?"

Krishna nodded.

"Woo hoo!"

"What? Oh shh."

"She is beautiful. Whoa."

Krishna started laughing. "I think you need to ask her out Julie, by the looks of it. How do you know her?"

"I met her at a ZBT party. She was with Ravi." Julie nodded, remembering.

Ravi was course 2 like Julie and they'd done a project together the year before. And since he was Sri Lankan it had been a vague but helpful initial point of reference for the two them, when Krishna had been a freshman.

"Oh. Ravi?"

"Have fun!" said Julie, already heading out.

*   *

"That was so nice. You are such a good cook!" Ashley was sitting on the bean bag in his room, finishing the red wine they had started with the food. She was wearing a shortish skirt that stayed close to her thighs, which were smooth in light tights.

"Not too hot? I was worried about that..." He asked.

"Hot? As in hot spicy? No, it was just right. Wow. So this is like home cooked Sri Lankan food?"

"What? As opposed to take out? I suppose it is by definition; since I cooked it."

"No, silly boy. I mean is this what you have at home, for dinner?" The chicken curry had faded her bright red lip-gloss, but he could still see the hint of blush high on her cheek bones.

"Oh, well yes, sort of. But we have more stuff. More dishes." He didn't even start to explain that this would be lunch, not dinner, at home.

"Sounds fabulous. You know what? I'm trying to decide if I should do my junior year abroad in Sri Lanka."

"Oh does Wellesley have a program?"

"No, it is through another college; but you can get a year's worth of credits for it. I'd learn a lot, and I know I'd just love the food."

He leant back, propped up on his pillows, glancing at the window pane for a moment. It was a little warmer today; there was a light drizzle instead of snow. Drops of water were falling, slowly, deliberately, it seemed, off the edge of the quarter open pane, onto the sill.

"And that is a good reason?" He sipped his wine, turning back to her.

"Well, I am interested in Sri Lanka. You know that." She sounded defensive. Reaching for her bag, she took out her lip stick, and re-did her lips with practiced ease, slowly pouting.

He nodded quickly. "Yes, of course."

"Krishna?"

He smiled almost unthinkingly.

"I was wondering... You are a sophomore right?"

He nodded again.

"So..." She stopped, small fingers pressed to bean bag. "You were there during these riots? I mean you were in Sri Lanka in 1983, right?"

"Yes I left right after the riots, at the end of August, to come here."

"You are... Tamil right?"

He seemed to stiffen. "How do you figure?"

She bit her lip. "I'm sorry, if that is rude to say. I'm sorry. I just figured from the question you asked at the talk. I mean I thought you implied it."

He nodded and smiled slightly, not wanting her to be sorry, not wanting to be tense. "Yes, I'm Tamil."

"The riots... must have been hard for you? Was everything okay with your family?" She got off the bean bag and sat by the edge of the bed, by his hip, her thighs pressed together, body half turned to him, watching his face.

The water was pooling on the sill now; tiny drops gathering, islands on the grimy white surface. Slowly he took his eyes off the little puddles, hardly realizing Ashley was sitting so close, wisps of her scented hair brushing his hip. His mind calmed as he ran his eye on the edge of her ear, and the cutting ache in the back of his head lessened.

"Yes, they were fine." He looked out of the window again, feeling his cheek vibrate, unable to stop the tiny persistent motion. Most people here who asked about '83 stopped there, and he was used to that. Usually the subject changed to some thing more pleasant, after a quick "Oh that's good!"

But she said nothing, listening, her body turning further, one knee on the bed now, bent, tiny slipper kicked off.

He turned to her again, trying to smile, hoping to compose his face.

"You were in Colum... bo?"

"Yes, I was at home. My father was away visiting a friend in another town. It was just my mother and sister at home, so we figured they should hide — and they did, in another house."

Ashley was leaning forward, her fingers on his upper arm.

"Every thing was fine, until there was that crazy frenzy on Friday."

She nodded. "Black Friday, right? When the Sinhala people in Colombo thought they'd been attacked by the Tamil Tigers, and attacked back?" She spoke softly.

Krishna could see five little puddles on the sill, swollen, bulging out, the surface tension of their outsides holding them in.

He closed his eyes and tried to focus his mind on the equations that governed that tiny, odd force of nature, going through the derivation in his head. He knew his lips were trembling.

"There were these five guys, Ashley, they were being chased by this huge crowd, and right at our wall, they were cornered."

"Oh my God."

"They bashed their heads on our wall, and then smashed their skulls with blocks of concrete from the pavement — the sidewalk — right by our house, right there, just broke their skulls in."

He kept the cold red wine on the sill, and tried to cover his eyes and cover his face with the back of his hand.

She kissed him as he cried, first his cheeks and cheek bones, her hair on his face, warming and enveloping him, and then on his lips licking and nibbling, whispering softly, "oh you poor baby... poor baby."

They must have lain there for a long time, and drifted off to sleep; when he half woke up, it was nearly 3:00 am and Ashley was in sweet slumber, her head resting on his chest, breasts pressing softly on his ribs. Krishna covered her in his comforter, and sat by the window until dawn, thinking of the red patches on the pink walls of his parent's house, the patterns of water on the sill, and changing colors of the winter's sky.

It was much later in the morning, the tray of coffee, eggs and toast he'd brought her, balancing on her knees, that she asked, "Krishna? So is it safe now in Sri Lanka?"

"I don't know." He shook his head. "Every thing's fine in the south, I think. I go crazy trying to get news some times. There isn't much in the *Globe* or the *New York Times*. So I just pounce on the *Island* when it comes." He grinned.

"So I could go there? It would be safe?"

"Oh sure." He said. "I worry about my parents, but you'd be fine. And, actually, I was thinking of taking my junior year off and going home."

"Oh that'll be nice!" Ashley smiled brightly.

*   *

When he saw her again it was more than a month later. She hadn't called, and he didn't really have her number. But that day their eyes met suddenly in the middle of the infinite corridor, and she went, "Krishna!"

He stopped, and she hugged him gently and kissed him on both cheeks. "How nice to see you!"

"Manuel?" she said softly, diffidently almost, tugging on the sleeve of the bearded guy, in army surplus fatigues she was with, making him turn towards Krishna. "This is Krishna, Manuel. He is from Sri Lanka."

While they shook hands, she said, "Manuel's from Nicaragua."

The Train from Batticoloa

Every time Kodituvakku took the train to Colombo, the cripple would be there, crouching on the metal platform between the coaches. His right arm was a claw. Thin and crooked, it moved across his body in jerky movements that matched the rhythm of the thrusting pistons. The moment the train stopped at a station, the cripple would crawl into the coach. Grinning, clutching his tin can he would rattle it at the new passengers. Kodituvakku always gave him twenty-five cents, and then the cripple would crawl away on his stubby thighs, veering sideways as he tried to move on.

After the CTF units had been stationed in Batticoloa, the trains would stay empty until Pollonaruwa. Only occasionally, when there was talk of a riot in Colombo, CTF units from camps all over the Batticoloa district would be recalled to the capital. Then they would fill up the train as it went through Pollonaruwa to Colombo. But today all through the long journey the wooden seats of the coach were nearly empty.

At the Pollonaruwa station the coach filled up with people traveling to Colombo. Kodituvakku leaned back and let the warmth of the Sinhala voices relax him. Families were settling down in clumps; mothers shooed their daughters into corners, fathers hoisted heavy bundles onto the overhead racks.

A bald man with bushy eyebrows helped his wife onto the train. Cautiously, the woman drawing up her sari as she passed the cripple, they made their way from the platform between the coaches to the seats. Stabbing his left arm into the floor with each backward jerk of his body, the cripple pulled himself into the corner. Here a grizzled man with lumpy skin unloaded a huge bag of chickens, then tucked up his sarong, shook out an ocher cloth and tied it around his head. The cripple crawled out from behind the sack crying out to the pious. A girl who had taken the seat next to Kodituvakku dropped a rupee in his can and the cripple got back to the platform.

Kodituvakku parted his thighs and rested his automatic rifle against his left leg. Slowly, his thumb moved down the barrel till it reached the catch that held in the bayonet. The girl looked at the insignia on his arm. Moving his arm away from his body Kodituvakku tightened his biceps. He caught her eye and smiled. She smiled back, narrowly, keeping her teeth hidden. Her red and white dress had ridden up over her knees, and her short hair blew in the wind from the open window. She was traveling alone.

"From where do you come, younger-sister?" Kodituvakku asked.

Her eyes flickered, as if considering something. "Meegamuwa."

He searched his mind for something to say, "You get good crabs there, don't you?"

"During the season." A delicately made sandal dropped off her foot.

"I know how to cook them. We get plenty of crabs in Batticoloa." When they didn't have any Tamil boys in the camp for interrogation, the Sergeant would have Kodituvakku cook crabs for the men.

"How you lie!" she said, laughing merrily. "Tell me how you do it."

He turned towards her. "First you get a beeg pot of water." The girl giggled. "Then," he pretended to think hard, "you get the crabs." The smile faded from his face. "While the water boils I hold the crabs over the boiling pot. I hold them by the claws. One claw in each hand. The first joint to break is the one at the end of the claw. When the big joint snaps the crab falls into the water. It crawls around while it cooks."

"You're very wicked. Don't you know it is a sin to kill animals?" She frowned, and then crossing her legs looked quizzically at Kodituvakku. "It is the only way to do it," Kodituvakku said a little too loudly.

The young woman said nothing.

"So are you traveling all the way to Colombo?" he asked, trying to start afresh.

'Yes, I go to the University."

Kodituvakku smoothed his mustache. "Aah! That is very good," he said. "One of my cousin-sisters is at the Kelaniya Campus. I also took my exams, and did very well, but I didn't go to the University. So, what is your name?"

"Sonali. What did you take your exam in?"

"Oh! The usual subjects..." He smiled. "I'm Kodituvakku."

Sonali looked away, pursing her lips.

The chickens were fighting inside the jute sack. Squirming desperately, the cripple tried to get out of the reach of the sharp beaks that pierced the brown weave.

The woman in the white sari was fanning herself with a newspaper. Sweat dripped down from her hair and split around the black mole on her cheek.

"This is the heat of the devil!" she exclaimed.

"I think the gods have cursed us for our sins— that is why the rains haven't come." The chicken farmer rubbed the gray stubble on his chin. "In the old days we would have asked the gods to help us, but now we do nothing, and wait for the government to banish the devils."

Kodituvakku grinned at the man's superstition. Sonali laughed — a soft delicate laugh. Kodituvakku caught her eye, and nodded. The woman gave Sonali an angry look.

"They say that the government will ask the monks to chant *pirith* at the Temple of the Tooth. Then the devils will be banished and the rains will come," she proclaimed.

"The whole country is going through an evil time," said her husband, "You talk of rain," he sniggered at his wife, "but this is not the real problem— let us do something about the Tamils, and everything will be all right."

His wife angrily poked at her straw bag with her umbrella. The farmer nodded.

"And what is the government doing?" The bald man went on. "Look at the Tamil devils: They are raping our women and eating our children— soon the Sinhala *jathiya* will be history. But tell us what is happening in Batticoloa," he addressed Kodituvakku respectfully.

75

A loose nail at the end of the seat rattled violently as the train ploughed through the still countryside. The fine particles of dust blowing in with the hot, dry wind scraped Kodituvakku's eyes.

"The Tigers are terrified of us," he said.

Sonali was looking at him; her eyes were large, knowing. "I thought the Tigers were giving you a lot of trouble?" she said, swiveling to and fro on her hips.

"That is just it— they never fight face to face. All they can do is set off a mine and run. They are cowards," he attempted a grin. "But we will get them in the end."

"How many of our army boys are with you, son?" the grizzled farmer joined the conversation.

"We are not the army." Kodituvakku said, lips curling upward.

"Is that so?" the farmer removed his head cloth and placed it on his shoulder. "Forgive my not knowing," he said humbly.

The train lurched, shifting the fine dust on the floorboards into new patterns. The jute sack rolled onto the cripple pinning him into the corner of the platform. He pushed back, using his good hand as a lever.

Kodituvakku displayed his insignia: "CTF. Central Task Force," he carefully enunciated the English words, while trying to catch Sonali's eye.

"There are only one thousand of us in the whole country." His voice grew rich as Sonali listened intently, "The Minister gave Batticoloa to us in '85 and we are going to keep it."

"And how are you going to do this?" Sonali asked raising her finely plucked eyebrows.

"Ah! You will not find it easy to understand our methods; we have had special training. We are not like these half-baked army fellows."

"Your training must have been harder than the University exams?" Sonali's face was a picture of seriousness.

Kodituvakku faltered.

"What is wrong with the army, arh?" The bald man knitted his bushy eyebrows. "My younger brother is in the Sinha regiment— they are every bit as good as you fancy men. What he says is that if they were given half a chance they could beat the Tamils with their little finger. But the government is soft on the Tamils."

"Why, only last week in Habarana the Tigers ate flesh and drank blood." The farmer interjected. "They say— I don't know if it is true— that red fire sprouted from their eyes. But one thing is certain; even the devil *Mahasona* has never been so cruel. They killed babies so young— the smell of their mother's milk was fresh in their mouths. Ah! What is the use of talking," his voice grew high-pitched streaming out of his nose, "We must do something now, or the Tigers will get us all."

"It is left to the God of Kataragama to save us," said the bald man. "The other gods are not strong enough."

"They say He helped the Kings of old drive the Tamils to the sea," added his wife after a respectful pause.

"Yes, He must give His power to our soldiers." The farmer looked at Kodituvakku.

"We are not afraid of these Tigers," Kodituvakku spoke calmly, but his Adam's apple moved with each word. "We are going through such a bad time because the army fellows messed things up."

"What does the army do wrong?" the bald man cracked his knuckles.

"Oh, when something happens, say a land mine goes off — they just go into town and burn and loot, and kill the people in the streets."

"So what? What else can they do?" The bald man's wife glanced at her husband.

"Yes, what I say is that we should have finished the Tamils off in '83. We left too many of them and see what is happening now."

"If we do this to them, they will pay us back," Sonali smiled demurely at the woman.

"You think that just because you've been to the University and read a few books you know everything: In my day well brought up young girls always traveled with their elders, and were respectful." The woman stabbed her umbrella into the floor.

The train slowed down; the sound of its engine died down to a whisper. Again the cripple tried to push aside the jute bag. Now and then it would slip back and he would start over. He moaned to himself calling upon the gods to save him.

"No, don't be too hard on her — she is right," Kodituvakku smiled and nodded at Sonali.

The bald man made a sharp, angry noise.

"Let me explain," said Kodituvakku. "If we get angry we can't do anything. Just killing people at random is wrong. There must be an order and a method to everything."

The train stopped. The air in the coach hung still and warm. The cripple crawled out from the platform moving his body from the hot, uneven metal plates to the cool smooth planks of the aisle.

Slowly Sonali shook her head. Her fingers played on her knuckles. "Explain your method to us," she turned to Kodituvakku. "We..." he began and broke off as the cripple started rattling his can.

"Why has the train stopped?" asked the bald man looking out of the window. No one answered. A distant rumble filled the air. The bald man pulled his head back. Fear was etched into the furrows on his brow. His hand was shaking.

"The Tigers?" his wife whispered.

"We are not far from the Habarana junction," the farmer wiped the sweat off his neck with
his cloth. His breath was shallow. Kodituvakku
moved to the edge of his seat. His hands went to his
gun.

"Isn't it just thunder?" asked Sonali. The
cripple was creeping towards her. There were pink,
raw marks on his back where the chickens had
pecked him. "*Aney*, it is a sin — his back is bleeding," she said, pulling out a small handkerchief.

"Don't look at him, *duva*," said the bald
man's wife. Hurriedly she pushed her bag under
their seat and raised her umbrella. "He will cast a
evil eye on you— you might even get possessed."

The cripple moved closer. His red, blood
shot eyes bulged out of his face. He reached out and
touched Sonali's ankle. She jerked backwards kick-
ing out.

"Get him out," the farmer screamed.

Kodituvakku grabbed the cripple by the
neck. "This is not a station," he said, "You can only
beg at a station. Get back," he gave him a shove.
The cripple drew back. From the corner of his eye
Kodituvakku could see the spasmodic jerking of his
stump.

Kodituvakku smoothed out his pants, and
repositioned his gun. The people settled down again;
they were calmer now. "What were we talking

about?" Kodituvakku asked rubbing his hands together.

"Ah! You asked about our method." He paused, "So it is like this. Every society needs rules. When too many people break these rules the society collapses. That is why we watch over the people. You see, we understand the rules, which is why we know what to do. Even if we make a few mistakes, it doesn't matter, because the rules are always right." He scraped the sweat off his brow. For a moment his lips kept moving silently. "Let me explain it again," he offered.

"No, no, that's very impressive," Sonali nodded. Her lips turned down and puckered slightly, "It must have taken you a long time to learn that— it is like the *bana* the priest preaches on a Poya-day," she laughed her soft delicate laugh. "When you've finished I will say *Sadhu, Saadhu*. Now, now don't get angry," she added hastily as Kodituvakku's lips hardened. "I was only joking."

"You see," he tried again, "society is like a train— it should run on its tracks not all over the place. A train stops at stations, people get on, the vendors sell their food and the beggars receive alms. Then the train leaves the station and goes on its way."

"Wait. Tell me what you actually do when something happens?"

"What do you mean?"

"You know, when a landmine blows up— what does the CTF do?" she tilted her head as though teasing, but her face darkened.

"These are not things to laugh about," Kodituvakku snapped. "Don't you understand? Haven't they taught you anything at the University?"

"No," she said slowly, "you can teach me much more than they can..."

Kodituvakku gripped the barrel of his gun. "All right, I'll tell you," he said, his voice like iron.

"We start early in the morning fanning out in Jeeps and trucks. We go to every village around the area of the blast. If you get there very early in the morning you can get all the men at once." He smiled slightly. "They try to run when they hear the Jeeps. When our unit first started operations some of them would actually get away. But now," he nodded slowly, "we drive in from all sides.

"We bring in all the young men, every one between sixteen and forty."

"Everybody?"

"We don't touch the women and children. Even though they run behind the trucks screaming at us. No, only the men. Yesterday was a good day— we got three hundred."

"And, then?"

"And then we interrogate them. That is all there is to it," Outside, in the distance, the dry

82

brown scrub lay still in the hot air. Sweat was trickling from Kodituvakku's wrist down to his palm.

Sonali stared at him, her mouth open. Her lower lip trembled. "I see... I see."

"There is no other way to do it. He lowered his voice so that the others wouldn't hear him, "We have to stop the landmines— You have never seen what they do to us." He looked down at the cracks on the wooden floor. "The day before yesterday it was my bunk mate Upul." He moved his damp fingers down the barrel of his gun, then, his thumb resting on the catch, rubbed them on the iron to rid them of sweat. "I am going to Colombo to give his ring to his wife."

Sonali edged away from him. She reached for her bag on the rack and gave it a vicious tug. Books scattered as the bag crashed to the ground.

Kodituvakku's thumb jerked. The bayonet shot out of the gun slicing through the leg of his fatigues. A single green thread cut across the shining steel tip of the bayonet. The people fell silent.

His hand shaking uncontrollably he tried to push the bayonet back into the gun. It took him a long time. "This always happens— the catch is loose" he said pushing back the beret that had settled over his eye.

Sonali got up and started collecting her books. The cripple crawled forward whimpering.

"I told you to get out," Kodituvakku yelled.

The cripple raised his head and stared at Kodituvakku with his bloodshot eyes. His mouth opened and his tongue hung out. He was screaming. The bald man's head snapped back hitting the window frame.

"God, he is possessed," wailed his wife pointing her umbrella at the cripple.

The cripple went on screaming. Quietly Kodituvakku got up. "Enough of this madness," he said. He bent down, clasped the cripple's thumbs and held them together in his clenched fist. Then, slowly he raised his fist holding the cripple high in the air.

His boots trampling on the pages of a notebook, he carried the cripple out of the coach.

There was a sharp dry sound like the snapping of a twig.

"What was that?" asked Sonali. The bald man brought his thumbs together, and cracked them again and again. No one spoke in the coach.

A short whimper broke the silence.

Sonali huddled in her seat, "it has got so cold suddenly," she said with a shudder.

"But it is so refreshing, after the heat," said the bald man lying back languidly on the seat.

His wife bent down to her straw bag at her feet. "We might as well eat if the train is going to be stuck here," she said as she brought out a comb of bananas. "Have one," she offered the others.

"Not for me," Sonali said backing away. Bending down she gathered her books from the floor, stuffed them into her bag, and rose to leave the coach.

She stopped at the entrance to the platform. After moment she drew back, and then slowly returned to her seat.

The bald man was the first to take a banana. "I think it is going to rain," he said holding his hand to the wind.

Again the rumble of thunder filled the air—louder and closer than before.

"Yes, it will rain." The farmer smiled as he skinned his banana. The train began to move towards Colombo. "We should not have been so frightened," he went on biting into his banana, "the gods will always watch over us."

A Man From Jaffna

"Ah! Yes, I've heard the bad news. Have some tea. Keeps you warm in this cold Boston weather. When was he taken in? Yesterday? Sugar? These Americans like it with lemon. So what has the boy been up to?" Mr. Sundar looked grave as he sipped his tea delicately. "This is too strong — some hot water Rani," he called to his wife.

"We don't quite know Mr. Shayam-Sundar. My mother called me up last night from Colombo — they want us to do something at this end." Suresh fidgeted in the overstuffed armchair. Actually it was his cousin Sonali who had called first, and then three times after, each time with a little more information. She had known before any one else, it seemed. He could still hear her voice, echoing in the distance at the end of the line, seeming to break into little bits as she said out loud, "They've taken him to Boosa."

"Yes, yes of course, we will do everything — you can be rest assured of that. Now, what is your brother's name?" Mr. Sundar settled down into a well-worn corner of the sofa across the room.

"Krishna."

Mrs. Sundar brought in the hot water, and put it on the coffee table. "What would you like for a snack?" she asked.

"Whatever you have Mrs. Shayam Sundar," Suresh hardly looked up.

"Your brother was here before he went back, didn't he?" Mr. Sundar asked.

"Yes, he was at MIT. He was here for three years; he is a junior. He took a leave of absence and went back." Biting his nails, Suresh looked around the room. An expensive TV and stereo, both protected with transparent covers, sat in two corners of the room. Bookshelves lined the walls, filled with leather bound classics that seemed brand new.

"Em. Eye. Tee. Shah! That is what I heard, nice to see our young Tamil boys doing well in the States. Do I know your father, son? What is his name?

"Yoganathan"

"Yoganathan... was he station master Hatton?"

"No, he is a doctor. Retired now. Krishna... Krishna is at the Boosa camp."

"Yoganathan... I can't seem to place the name — what is your village in Jaffna?"

Suresh bit his lip. His finger nails dug into his palm, he hated this question, always. "I can't quite remember the name of the village, somewhere near the town I think — but I was born in Colombo."

"Ah! Colombo ... You are almost like my daughter." Sundar shook his head sadly. "She can't even speak Tamil — she speaks English with an American accent." Sundar dusted the air with his hands, plump fingers flicking forward. "What I always say is this — we are all Tamils, isn't that so, son."

Suresh nodded vigorously.

"You see what I mean—that is the meaning of our struggle."

Suresh cleared his throat. "What I am very worried about is torture, Mr. Sundar. They must have started on him." Suresh lifted his eyes. "Please, if you could contact someone in the State Department, they might ask our government to go easy on him." On the wall above Mr. Sundar's chair was a framed, autographed photograph of Senator Edward Kennedy and Mr. Sundar. Light bounced off the glass into Suresh's eyes.

"Terrible things are happening, son, people being picked up off the streets, tortured in the camps. But our boys have vowed to fight to the end. Tell me, did I meet your brother when he was here? I'm sure I'd remember him. What does he look like?"

Suresh pulled out a photograph of Krishna, rowing on the River Charles.

"Looks like a fine boy," admired Mr. Sundar, "I don't seem to remember the face though ... I wonder if he came to any of our meetings." He looked quizzically at Suresh.

"Meetings... ? Ah! Yes the Association."

"You know the Tamil Eelam Association meetings," Mr. Sundar went on as if he hadn't heard. "We have them once a month."

"I know. I know. About Krishna; Mr. Sundar, do you think..."

"You young people should come to our meetings, so that we can get to know you."

"I've been a bit busy with school but I will try to come next month."

"Good good, you mustn't forget what's happening at home while you are here, you know." Suresh was about to speak, when Mr. Sundar held up his hand. "That is what I always say, even if we are here we can do some little thing, even if it is a small thing we must do it. When some of us come abroad, and I don't mean you, of course — I'm sure

you are not like this, still some people want to forget everything. But what I say is, a Tamil is a Tamil
wherever he goes. The important thing for us is our
family, our relatives, our people; after all what is a
man without his people?

Sundar settled in his chair again, thighs
scissoring slowly.

"That is what all the people said when we
first wanted to start the Association. 'What can you
do from here?' they said. 'Don't make trouble,' they
said. 'It won't work in the States' they said. But I
knew that our people were here, so I knew we
wouldn't have any trouble taking it forward: My
brother and two of my cousin-brothers are here,
and also Rani's people.

"That is why the Association did well —
look how far we have come. The Senators listen to
us. Next year, if everything is going like this I'm going to get my parents down from Jaffna.

"Now when anything happens at home the
first people to call me are the same big-shot doctors
and professors who were telling us to keep quiet.

"Not that I'm taking any credit for anything. As I was telling Senator Kennedy the other
day, I am waiting for someone to take over and run
the Association — there is a lot of work to be done;
talking to all these Senators, Congressmen, Amnesty
International. Then suddenly someone wants political asylum. I'm on the phone all night. I'm an old

man; and I have to run my shop during the day. Not that I regret the time I've been putting in, after all it's all for the cause — the cause comes first."

"I typed up lots of information about Krishna last night." Suresh pulled out a folder.

"Yes, yes, please leave it here. I will do everything I can; I will talk to Senator Kennedy first thing in the morning."

Sundar leaned back, and glanced at the logo on the folder. "So, you are at Boston College, arh son? Scholarship? This is a wonderful country, opportunity for every one — that is what I always tell my daughter, Devi. Study hard and you will go far, but I don't know she is never at home, never at her books, and the bad language she uses... but she is a good girl really." He paused. "Did you get in to BC straight from Ceylon?"

"Yes."

"This year?"

"Yes, I came last year, in the Fall of '86. I'm a freshman, this is my first year, '86-87."

"What were your SAT scores, if you don't mind my asking."

"Not very good." Suresh squirmed. "Krishna's were really good though. He is the bright one in the family." Suresh managed a half smile; flipped through the folder and found a sheet. "His were 710 verbal, 750 maths. Math, they say here."

"Good good, that is very good, no?" Sundar paused. "I say son, what is your mother's father's name?"

"Ratnasabapathi"

"Not the Civil Servant?"

Suresh nodded.

"He was secretary to the treasury, tall, fair…"

Suresh nodded again.

Sundar looked up, eyes widening. "Then you are Arunachalam QC's great-grandson."

Suresh looked down, almost embarrassed.

Sundar slapped the table. "I knew it, I knew it," He sang out, "you have the look of a Manipay boy, I can tell the face-cut any where. Why then we are connected through my wife's people; you see her cousin is married to your mother's uncle Gunam. They are in Canada, and doing very well.

"Rani," he called out to his wife, who came in carrying a plate of *vadais*, "this is Arunachalam QC's great-grandson!"

"No!? And not telling us. Shah! Living so close by — to think we didn't know. You are Kamala's son?"

"No, that is my aunt." Suresh smiled. "My mother is Pathma."

"Pathma's younger son. That is the thing! I've carried you when you were a baby, back home, those days, you don't remember. You were tiny!"

93

Mrs. Sundar sat down wiping her hands on her sari. A warm smile creased her face. "How you have grown-up, you must meet Devi — she should be coming back any time now."

"He's won a scholarship to BC...," Sundar offered Suresh more *vadai.*

"That side of the family has always been very academic." Rani nodded slowly.

"It is not quite a scholarship," said Suresh softly, "just financial aid."

"What ever it is I'm glad one of our people is getting it."

"You must stay for dinner — I'm making *thosai,*" Rani beamed at Suresh "How do you manage for food? You must be missing your mother's cooking — come by any time for a meal."

"That would be very nice, thank you." Suresh's tense face softened.

Rani went back to the kitchen. "To think I didn't know you were one of our boys — you should have told me," Mr. Sundar said reproachfully.

Mr. Sundar picked up the folder from the table; he read it carefully, his eyes contracting with the effort. "A fine boy," he said at last, "what a waste. I will do every thing I can," Sundar face was serious, drawn, "We will apply maximum pressure on the government. Have you talked to his professors at MIT?"

Suresh nodded. "I was going to."

"Very good. Talk to all the big shots there. There is no time to write letters. Tell them to telex, and cable. The best way is direct to the Minister of National Security, and the President — you have the addresses? And I will call our people in London and Delhi right away.

"And another thing, the Finance Minister is coming to Washington next week for a World Bank meeting — I will ask Senator Kennedy to speak to him personally. Can you get a group of your friends to go down to Washington next week, to demonstrate in front of our embassy when the Minister is there. Get some... some... American boys — it always helps. And of course, get people to write to the Senator.

"Don't worry," Sundar's mouth set in a hard line, "we will get him out in a month. They should never have touched one of our people."

Mr. Sundar patted his belly and stretched. "This must be such a hard time for you *thambi*," he said. "Would you like a beer?" And then glancing at the kitchen door he whispered. "Or, we can have some thing stronger, if you like."

"No, a beer will be fine, Uncle," said Suresh.

After two beers they sat down to dinner. Devi hadn't come home.

"The only thing is," Sundar said between bites of *thosai*, which he ate with a fork, "Will he come out if given the chance?"

"I don't quite get what you mean..." Suresh said.

"You know once before there was a case like this, a boy had been taken in on suspicion, no charges of course — he had studied abroad, and had friends in England — so they let him out on the condition that he left the country for good and kept out of trouble."

"I don't think Krishna would agree to that...," said Suresh slowly.

"So, what was this boy doing at home?" Mr. Sundar's eye narrowed.

"Oh! He was in Colombo."

"But what was he doing in Colombo?"

"I think he was going for some meetings with a group."

"What kind of group?"

"It is people from different areas I think. Some people from Colombo..."

"Sinhala group?" Mr. Sundar cut in.

"No, Sinhala and Tamil. Some Sinhala boys, and some Tamil boys, from Batticoloa, I think."

"Boys from Batticoloa are one thing son, but this sounds like a Sinhala group. The leaders are Sinhala right?"

"Yes."

"A Sinhala underground group. Marxist. There are several, I've heard." Sundar's lips were pressed together.

Suresh nodded. "Yes, I think. I never understood Krishna's politics properly, but he used to always say that the Tamil boys should join the Sinhala boys and fight together against injustice."

"Ah! Fight! What did he want to do? Let me tell you *thambi* — not that I have anything against the Sinhala people. But these Sinhala groups in Colombo are all fronts for the Communists. They are fine to use if you want to put pressure on the government, but that is all. They will kill all of us before they are done."

"But Krishna used to say this is… this whole conflict… is a… a class thing."

"But that is the wrong attitude, no? Oh, why on earth didn't this boy come and talk to me before he went rushing off to start the Revolution. All you intelligent boys don't understand these things properly, no? This is the thing. There are plenty of people to do the fighting there, you know," Mr. Sundar's voice dropped, "You know… these ordinary boys. They make good fighters mind you, best fighters in the whole world, but everybody doesn't have to fight you know. It is here that we need people — no? — that's what I say every day, educated boys from good families — like you and your brother — then we can talk to the Senators properly." And the other thing, what about our families, if all the young boys are going to be so hot headed, go to fight like this?

"A boy like you who has done so well will understand." He pointed expansively to the corners of the room, "we are just coming up in this country, not wealthy or anything like some of those big shot doctors in New Jersey, but doing fairly well, a car, a house — I saved up quite a bit for Devi's dowry." He smiled to himself, "we never saved any thing at home when I was a clerk in the income tax department. But it can all be ruined... let me tell you what happened to one of my good friends in California.

Sundar drew close to Suresh. "...Just when they were looking around for someone for their daughter, she had done well at Stanford, pretty girl, very pretty — they had almost fifty thousand saved up for dowry I hear — she went off with one of these..."

Sundar broke off in mid-sentence as the front door opened, and Devi walked in.

"Oh hi Dad." She said, seemingly surprised he was there. She glanced at the big clock behind her father, eyes shifting back to his face too quickly. She lifted a toe, the heel of her right pump digging into the carpet.

"This is Suresh, Devi. He is Arunachalam QC's great grand son."

"Who?"

Sundar mumbled, trying to explain. Suresh stepped forward, hand out stretched.

"Nice to meet you. Dad, I'm beat, Ok? G'night." Devi ran up the stairs, not looking back.

At the Water's Edge

"And what will you have?" asked Iqbal.

Iqbal had his right arm half lifted, half pointing, as if the gesture itself would produce a drink. It was a movement he used often, and not just for drinks. A waiter arrived quickly, as they always did at the Boating Club, in a buttoned white jacket and long dark pants, standing half turned, at the end of Iqbal's hand.

"Gray goose martini, straight up, dry," said Krishna.

His eyes moved from Iqbal's face to the waiter's, and back to Iqbal's watching as his friend's red-flecked eyes flickered.

"What the fuck is that, *machang*?" grunted Iqbal, knowing well what it was. "This isn't New York. Have a proper drink."

Siddha who was sipping a coke with a straw laughed prettily, but nervously and looked at Krishna.

"Bring this gentleman a Black Label, and another for me" Iqbal pushed the waiter off, with a flick of his ha

Krishna smiled and shrugged his shoulders, like it didn't matter. Actually he missed his gray goose vodka, but then again, being back home made you appreciate scotch, which is all Iqbal ever had, single malt when he was in New York and had a new credit card, Black Label at home. He looked again, at the fellow's face, seeing spots he had missed shaving, and darkening skin on the sides of his eyes. The mustache dropped over the thick upper lip, trying vainly to cover the oversized teeth.

"So did you watch the match?" Krishna asked.

"The boys aren't doing too well are they?" Iqbal sniggered.

This Krishna conceded. Sri Lanka had lost two tests and four one-dayers in South Africa. Today had been the last game. Lost again.

"But the commentary is really bad, isn't it?" asked Krishna.

"So biased, no?" Siddha nodded hard. "They are all just telling for their side."

Krishna agreed, face bland, keeping his wince at her syntax well inside. "Just a bunch of racists. It is all about us being children and having to learn the game. They always know the game already, supposedly."

"Yes, but it was just bad technique — our buggers can't bat" said Iqbal. "The commentary doesn't have any thing to do with that."

"Technique, becknique! That is what all the good old college buggers said when Sanath opened. Doesn't have the technique. But he got there, didn't he?"

The drinks arrived, and were set on the table.

"Just look at his record now —more sixes than any one ever, in the history of one day cricket." Krishna took his drink, and a deep breath knowing Iqbal didn't need a lecture on C. L. R. James. Iqbal knew what he knew, they had both read the same books, and fought the same fights in graduate school in New York. When they had finished, Iqbal had returned home, to teach English at Colombo.

Iqbal nodded, not saying any thing, his expression conceding the point.

"Cheers." He said, and sipped.

"What was that line of Rhumi's, Catti liked so much?" Krishna asked, knowing Iqbal knew, remembering his presence fresh and loud in that graduate seminar. He was trying to forget Catti, who'd taught it.

"Not quite, not white." Iqbal said, and sipped again, too soon. He rubbed his lips together and nodded, with an air of finality.

Krishna sipped also, nodding, yet stilling his head, stopped short at the quickness of his win. Sometimes he thought he was too sharp with Iqbal, thrusting back too forcefully, breaking his shell. But Iqbal always came back later, Krishna remembered, as the drink moved through him.

He turned and looked at Siddha. She lowered her eyes, shifting her slim body in the cane chair shyly, yet half invitingly, sensing he was looking her over. The young woman's delicate features were carefully made-up, and the hair styled, but not too fashionably. But her pants were tight and low, and the top cropped. Krishna smiled at her, thinking she had done well with the Iqbal-Injunction, "keep the *salwars* at your mothers!" It sounded crass when he had repeated it to Krishna, later, in the new apartment he and Siddha had rented, but he was chuckling happily, and she hadn't seemed too displeased at all. But she hadn't budged from coke, even to white wine or sherry, even though Iqbal had pressed her.

"So what did you think of Chandrika's speech Siddha?" He knew that was worth asking, since she followed politics closely, and had a lot to say, in general.

"As a feminist, I have problem with her," said Siddha.

"Oh?" asked Krishna, not quite getting it, but happy to hear more.

"You don't?" asked Siddha, her tone a little sharp.

Krishna ducked, letting that one sail past. "Don't... ?" he trailed off, asking.

"Don't have problem with her?"

"I'm not a feminist, Siddha," said Krishna chuckling.

She looked at Iqbal and then looked at Krishna, as if someone had lied to her. "I thought because you had got your pee etch dee like Iqbal, you understood these things."

Krishna laughed, thinking she was joking. "Oh no, I don't understand half the things Iqbal does."

"Iqbal is a feminist," she said insistently, not smiling at all.

Krishna sobered his expression.

"Is he now?" Krishna said eyes gliding over the lake, trying not to look at Siddha.

The beautiful, floodlit lawns of the Boating Club, which sloped down to the water, were dotted with tables where members sat in small groups while white-jacketed waiters scurried about. Krishna had first seen the Boating Club, when he had taken up rowing in school. If you wanted to row for King's, then you had to turn up for practices at the Boating Club. It was the only extracurricular thing Krishna could do, not having the reflexes for cricket, or the body for rugby, so he had tried out and worked at it, and then finally, when he had learnt the rhythm of rowing he had begun to crave it like a drug. He would come early for practice, just before dawn, and take the boat out, and sit in the water, almost still, gray in the first light of the morning, and imagine the boat flying across the surface, slicing it open.

But he had always hated the club; way back then he didn't know why, he just did. Now with his pee etch dee, as Siddha put it, he knew why. It was just what it shouldn't be. Krishna was sure it had been whites-only until quite late; there weren't any Sri Lankan names on the wall for the Madras-Colombo regatta, until 1962. And now, still, membership was not so much expensive as exclusive. Iqbal was a member; it was his favorite place to drink.

When Krishna looked down at his glass it was empty and Iqbal was saying, "Another round" in a way that brooked no argument.

"Sure" said Krishna.

"Sorry, Siddha... you were saying about Chandrika...?" Turned to her again, feeling like he had cut her off.

"As a woman, she should do more for gender," said Siddha, as if this was so obvious, and he was quite dense.

Perhaps it was, Krishna thought to himself. Siddha, he knew, was focused on gender. She worked as some kind of grant administrator with one of the European development aid agencies in Colombo that was into gender sensitizing and grass roots empowerment. Now, like everyone else, they had moved into something they called capacity building, funding every one and their sister. He didn't want to sneeze at her work though; she had said once that she woke up each morning, and craved to go into work, and it had given him pause, knowing how untrue that would be for him. "That's great Siddha," he recalled saying, "I can't say that for myself."

"I suppose she should, Siddha," he said as if he had considered her claim about the President's speech carefully, mulled it over, and seen her point. "But then she has that fellow, what's his name, in her Cabinet, right? And he's openly gay. Isn't that sort of encouraging?"

"These gays have to behave properly, no?" said Siddha, turning that one on its head. "Yesterday, one of these gays came to our office, and played hell. He wants to start some NGO, and was bringing a proposal. We were all laughing and laughing in the bathroom," Siddha recalled and laughed again, with a subtle twist of her torso, one hand covering her mouth with splayed fingers, red lips peeking through, tossing her dark locks back.

When Iqbal had first met Siddha, and that was only a few months ago — they had been introduced by one of Siddha's girl-friends, Vasi, who'd thought to match make — and he had proposed to her, he had emailed Krishna this one line, which he did not quite get at the time, "She flirts in such a primitive way, *machang*."

Sitting at the edge of the water of the Boating Club, on the well cut green lawn, seeing Siddha laugh, he got it. Krishna ran his thumb on his glass, glad it wasn't empty.

"What were you laughing at?" asked Krishna, feeling like he should say more, not knowing how quite to say it.

"The way he was doing his hands, men..." Siddha did her hands, well polished nails pointed at the end of her long fingers, palm curved, pushing the air. "And he was dressed in this shawl..." She giggled again.

Iqbal was looking away.

Krishna took a deep breath, not wanting to say too much. "But it is a human right to be different, right, Siddha. I mean, you wear what you want, he wears what he wants, right?"

She looked taken aback, as if human rights were another thing altogether, and he was confused.

"No, no." she said, "I'm not saying in Human Rights." She said it with the capitals.

"But it is a gender issue, isn't it?" Krishna was flailing. He cast a rather desperate look at Iqbal, who had his arm lifted, flexed, waiting for a waiter who was bringing a food menu. He didn't seem to see the look in Krishna's eye.

"I don't like my brothers to behave like that," said Siddha almost huffily, "that is what I am saying."

"Right, right," agreed Krishna, thinking the whole discussion was going to become undrinkable, rather too soon.

Iqbal had the dinner menu at the edge of his hand, pincered between two fingers like a long, wide cigarette. His arm was raised. The waiter was attentive, waiting for the order.

Krishna knew with hardly a thought that he would have the lamb chops, knowing that would be Iqbal's choice as well. But Siddha still needed to consult the menu, and she did, carefully, before selecting the grilled chicken breast.

When they were in New York, and he cooked, Iqbal would regularly demand he make pork chops. The first time, Iqbal had accompanied him to the supermarket, and pointed out the ones he wanted. And then was very clear how he wanted them done. "Add pineapple, and that Worcestershire sauce. Then add sugar...." Krishna had wanted to

108

ask why he didn't make it himself, but then even though he had known him for years, he just couldn't. But after he had slaved over it, Iqbal had declared it quite good, just needing a little of this and that, next time. Then he'd finished off several chops, leaving the designated bottle of single malt supine; every so often, he would return for more. Krishna, grinned, remembering, and turned to Siddha, thinking it would be fun to tease Iqbal, by telling her the tale. But in a flash he caught himself, and stopped.

"Have another drink," said Iqbal, lifting his hand. Krishna acquiesced, murmuring and then articulating his protests. Iqbal may have had a couple while he waited, and another seemed to have worked its way through the delivery system, unheralded, while Krishna was nursing his. So was that four or five? There was no check on this, since only Iqbal could order here; only Iqbal was a member. But it wasn't the tally of who paid for what that mattered, it was how many he had. Krishna knew this was a problem, not just for his liver, but also for his wife. "Going out everyday and boozing," Siddha had complained to her girl-friend, who had of course called up Krishna at once. "You advise him," she had said, "otherwise, he won't listen."

"Ok, one last one before dinner," Krishna said pleasantly, drumming his fingers on the armrest of the chair, knowing he was clean out of advice.

"I've been cutting back on my drinking, *machang*, can't put them back like in the old days."

Iqbal sipped his drink, once, and then again, raising the glass, to examine the level of the liquid, as if that mattered a great deal. He moved his lips; preparing to say something he needed time to think through.

Someone from the next table walked by, grinning, hand out to Iqbal, hailing him, as if long lost. "Hey hey ...so you are back?" The man, thumped Iqbal on the back as he stood, and they chatted, as college buggers do, about nothing at all. "Oh last year... teaching... here? ...Peradeniya? Ahh... Colombo. Good. Good." They shook hands again, as the man said, "See you later, Imthiaz," and turned, still smiling as he walked away.

Krishna looked up as Iqbal sat down. "Did that guy call you Imthiaz?"

Iqbal nodded, laughing, his right shoulder shaking, arm not fully extended, but still away from his body.

"You should have slapped him," Krishna said softly looking at Iqbal's hand.

Iqbal still had a smile on his face, but his hand was back on his drink, holding it. He then lifted the glass and looked at it again, as if he had now worked out what he needed to say. "You were never much of drinker, ever." He was no longer smiling.

Krishna, stopped, his mind still and cold. There was a noise in the water, of slight splashing, and then a faint ripple of movement.

Iqbal said what he said calmly, deliberately, as if it was well considered by the jury, and all the evidence had been weighed. He said it like it mattered, and mattered a lot, as a matter between men.

"Well," said Krishna, voice thinning. "I remember finishing a bottle in an evening, you and I together." He stopped, unable to change the pitch of his voice.

Siddha filled the silence.

"You know, Krishna, this is what I have been telling Iqbaal," said Siddha, dragging out the vowel in his name cutely. "It is not good for him. He should realize himself no, he has studied and all."

Krishna withdrew, gladly, regaining his composure, as Siddha entered the lists, more flatly than her finely strapped, pencil-heeled sandals might allow.

The food arrived, allowing comments to be reserved.

"So what are you teaching?" asked Iqbal, as the salt and pepper went round.

Krishna was pleased he asked, for this was the first time he had asked in the three weeks Krishna had been back, the first time Iqbal had really mentioned Krishna's year old job, the job of the year, that he had landed at Harper University.

"Oh... yes, I designed this grad. seminar, "Anthropology of Violence." Krishna got enthusiastic, as he explained, fingers forming the argument of the class on an imaginary potter's wheel in front of him. Iqbal nodded, asking good questions, cutting his chops, when Krishna realized that Siddha may not be getting much of this, since it was deep in some unpackable container of knowledge.

"I was teaching this class, Siddha," he said, turning to her trying to rearrange the ideas in his head in a different way for her.

Siddha broke in. "When I teach, I always give the note first," she said. "That makes it easy."

"Oh? What do you teach?"

"When we do gender training. Training the trainers."

Krishna turned to his chops, making up for lost time.

"No Siddha, this is a seminar Krishna is talking about. It is all discussion." Iqbal nodded, his arm chopping the air, slowly, his chin pointed towards Siddha.

"Oh, I'm sure the students wish they had some sort of notes dictated to them," Krishna said letting a smile drift into his voice, fork lifted, glancing at Siddha. "Anyway, it went well. Even Rhumi got wind of it, and I made his dinner list."

"So you know him?" There was tinge of something in Iqbal's matter of fact tone.

"No... no... well... yes... He is there, you know." Krishna stumbled, just looking at Iqbal. Rhumi Bhabhler was at Harper, in the way Catti Mukkerjee-Goldstein was at Greenwich. Or at least, that is how people said it.

"But you know how these people are..." Krishna was trying to back out. "It is all just some kind of a two step." He stopped and deadpanned. "They all just want to go to Harvard and die."

Iqbal grinned, "Or die and go to Harvard," he said, and sipped his drink, as if he had said nothing.

Krishna cracked up with Iqbal, side shaking with laughter.

As he settled down, dabbing his lips with his napkin, Siddha asked, "Do you have sisters, Krishna?" He put down the napkin, refolding it in a triangle for some reason, feeling he needed to say more about the class.

"One, she is much younger to me, perhaps you would know her." Krishna considered, thinking his sister was Siddha's age. "Rudikala... Rudikala Yoganathan," he stopped, waiting for Siddha to reflect if she did know her. "Maybe you've seen her around... She was at Queen's," he added helpfully.

Siddha looked blank. "Queen's," he said again, thinking he wasn't being clear somehow, "right next to King's, where Iqbal and I went."

"On Racecourse Avenue?"

113

Krishna nodded, not knowing what to say. The two floodlights at the edge of the water were attracting those tiny brown insects that they always did. He knew they were buzzing, crashing against the glass of the lights, but from where they sat, all was quiet, except for the soft, polite murmur of voices at the tables.

Iqbal jumped in, "Have you read Balibar's new book?"

"I started, yes."

Iqbal went on, explaining what he got out of it, what was wrong with it, and so on, summarizing with great finesse. And Krishna listened, making mental notes, leaning back.

Iqbal was still a bigger Marxist than he was a drinker, his seminar papers in graduate school always starting off with Lenin, and working through to Althusser. But then he had discovered feminism, or some variant of it, and the two had combined, like a fist, hard and strong, that you felt in the pounding sentences of his essays, as some novelist or historian, who wouldn't know and wouldn't care, was beaten and bashed, again and again, until you felt Iqbal was done.

"There are two sides to politics," Iqbal was explaining Balibar to him "constitutional politics and insurrectionary politics."

"I see." Krishna, nodded as he listened, thinking he needed to spend more time with French

114

Marxism. Of late, he hadn't, only remembering Marxism when he was reminded of it. As Vasi, Siddha's girlfriend had, just two weeks ago, calling him, and just announcing, with cold anger, "All you Marxist men. You are all bastards." He had felt his throat go dry at her tone, his mind warm and confused, trying, somehow and suddenly, to remember to forget. "Marxist?" he said at last, voice barely audible. "Yes" she snapped, "Like you, Iqbal and Piyal... " She trailed off, and Krishna began to get where she needed to go. Piyal and Vasi had been very much together, very much in love, before a bitter break up. And he and Piyal, were two of those guys who had got involved and got arrested, because, supposedly, every one said, they were too macho and too Marxist to stay clear.

Krishna tried to stop his thoughts, moving his finger over his forehead. He cradled the phone between his ear and shoulder, while walking to the fridge, and reached for a bottle, feeling the cool of its heaviness in his palm and fingers, as he sat down, pouring into a tall glass. The water swirled and the glass clouded. They hadn't got Iqbal, and he'd stayed underground some how, keeping in touch with Sonali, and moving mountains with Suresh, who had been in Boston, to get Krishna out.

Vasi was steaming on. "Look at the way he is treating Siddha!" she exclaimed. "He is a such a bastard."

"Tell me what he has done." Krishna asked, quietly, calmer now. And she went on and on, about his "boozing" not hearing Krishna when he pointed out that Iqbal had been drinking a lot forever. "I mean, that is the way he is, Vasi," he had tried.

"Let him kill himself, but why should he spend her money?" she countered.

"Her money?" Krishna asked, the anthropologist in him trying to grasp the details of the thing. It turned out that Siddha earned more than Iqbal, since she was with an aid agency that simply paid on a different scale. But with apartment rents being what they were, it wasn't all that, if you wanted to live where Iqbal wanted to live in the city. And Siddha wanted to give a good part of her salary to her widowed mother.

"He should support her, no, without taking her money. I thought he was a feminist."

Krishna could feel Vasi shaking her head. "Half her salary to her mother?" Krishna said cautiously, considering. "I don't know Vasi, I think couples always have to work out these things. Money is such a tough one, until you work it out, isn't it?" Vasi would have none of that. "He should understand as a feminist," she insisted. She'd gone from Marxism to feminism, and he knew it was all clear as it could be to her. "Yes, all right," he said. "I'll try to talk to him... I think, though, may be, they need to see a counselor or some one, right?"

He tried one last time, hanging on before she hung up.

The one time Iqbal had spoken of his mother-in-law to Krishna it was with such pleasure. "She and I," he had said, "understand each other." And of course, that meant something to Iqbal since Siddha's mother didn't speak English, and Iqbal hardly spoke Tamil.

Krishna had never met Siddha's mother, but he knew she'd had a hard time. Siddha's family had been expelled from their homes in the North by the Tigers, in a terrifying moment of viciousness, about 6 or 7 years ago now. Towards the end of nineteen ninety, the Tigers, literally on one fine day, had simply asked the Muslims who'd lived among the Tamils, and who had so lived for generations and generations, who spoke Tamil and nothing else, really, except for when they prayed, to pack up and get out. But it had been awhile now, and he didn't think Siddha's family was really badly off any more.

But he didn't know.

Krishna moved his fingers through his hair, fingers splayed. The air was still and damp, after the rains, and felt too warm. The food waiter was clearing the plates, and he'd left the bill in the leather fold. Iqbal signed it, leaving a note half sticking out of the covers, as a tip. Krishna could see Siddha glancing down at the 500. Iqbal had his arm lifted, waiting for the drinks waiter, who would bring a separate bill.

"England will be here soon, right?" Krishna asked quickly.

"Yes, next month," Iqbal nodded.

"I think I'll just make the third test, before I leave."

Iqbal nodded.

"They've done up CSC bar, did you know? Plate glass windows, AC, leather seats. You can watch the whole match from in there now." Now a days, the third test was always at the CSC. It hadn't always been, but now, after Ranatunga had discovered Jayasuriya's potential and had for a magic moment, taken over cricket in Sri Lanka, it was. And Krishna kept up his membership there, just for that reason. And now, they'd upgraded.

"Oh really?" asked Iqbal.

"Yes, I went in last week, just to check it out."

The waiter brought the drinks bills, which Iqbal scanned and signed. He left another two crisp 500s in the bill-fold. Iqbal always tipped excessively; if asked he maintained he did it to get good service, but Krishna didn't believe it was all about utility. Iqbal smiled at the waiter, as he gave him back the billfold.

"Thank you Anura." The waiters at the Boating Club didn't wear name tags.

"OK, then?" Iqbal stood up, rubbing his hands together.

Krishna stood as well. "Thanks very much, *machang*. It is so quiet and cozy here, isn't it?" He looked around, at the well spread out tables.

Iqbal laughed, and slapped him hard on his shoulder, with his right hand. "Yeah, not like the CSC — they haven't let in all those buggers who went to Dharmaduta, and god knows where else, here. Just chaps from King's and St. Luke's."

Krishna winced, but not from the blow on his back. He looked at Siddha — who was standing now — trying to see her face in the shadowy light, wondering what she had heard.

In the distance, the water rippled, and there was a splash. A water monitor, dark, scaly, was cutting though the water, splitting it, with its glistening jaws just above the surface, speeding through. Then the water was still, and utterly quiet again.

Krishna looked at Siddha's face one more time, and slowed his steps, falling back, crossing his arms softly and tightly, following the two of them as they walked out of the club.

Glossary.

6-3	A computer science major (MIT-speak)
Amma/i	Mother (Sinhala)
Ayubowan	Greetings; lit.: a wish of long life (Sinhala)
betel/*bulath*	Leaf; masticated as a stimulant (English/Sinhala)
coq au vin	French dish; chicken with wine
course 2	A mechanical engineering major (MIT-speak)
d&d	Dungeons and dragons
Dheepavali	Hindu Holiday (Tamil)
dorai	Master/boss (Tamil)
duva	Young girl; lit. daughter (Sinhala)
hunu	White wall paste; Calcium Carbonate
jathiya	Race or kind (Sinhala)
machang	Term of intimacy among men; lit.: brother-in-law (Sinhala & Tamil)
madama	Orphanage (Sinhala)
mahathaya	Gentleman; lit. man of good qualities (Sinhala)
nona	Lady (Sinhala)
pirith	Aural Buddhist ritual (Sinhala)
Resnick & Halliday	A physics text book
salwar	Long loose cotton blouse, and loose pants, worn with a shawl (Hindustani)
sophomore	2nd year student in a US university
thaali	Marriage necklace (Tamil)
thambi	Young fellow; lit. younger brother (Tamil)
thosai	Crepe, made of lentil batter (Tamil)
thotta kadu	Garden/plantation (Tamil)
vadai	Fried lentil cake (Tamil)
WASP	White, Anglo-Saxon, Protestant
watte	Shanty complex; Lit. garden (Sinhala)
ZBT	All male living group; MIT fraternity

Acknowledgements

First, if you've read this book through, I'd like to thank you for it. I like to think I've reached you, for a moment, where ever you may be, and I hope to do better next time.

Many many people have read these stories, in different versions over the years, and their critical comments have helped me write better. Among them are Kumari Jayewardena, Regi Siriwardena, Katherine Burnette and Malathi de Alwis; I thank them all for the care of their attention.

I owe my long, tough relationship to the written word to my mother, who taught me to read and write and shared with me, in so many ways, her love of books. I thank her for that gift of letters.

My greatest debt is to Illona Karmel, without whom, I would never, ever, have finished a story. This collection, belated and old, is for her.

Pradeep Jeganathan was born in Colombo in 1965 and was educated at Royal College, MIT, Harvard and Chicago where he earned a doctorate in cultural anthropology. He has written extensively on the anthropology of violence, and has taught anthropology at Chicago, the New School's Graduate Faculty and at the University of Minnesota, where he was McKnight-Land Grant Professor in 2000-2002. He is now a Senior Fellow at the International Centre for Ethnic Studies in Colombo and edits the Centre's scholarly journal *Domains*.

Printed in the United States
23942LVS00005B/36